Forever Friends

forever friends

A Novel

LYNNE HINTON

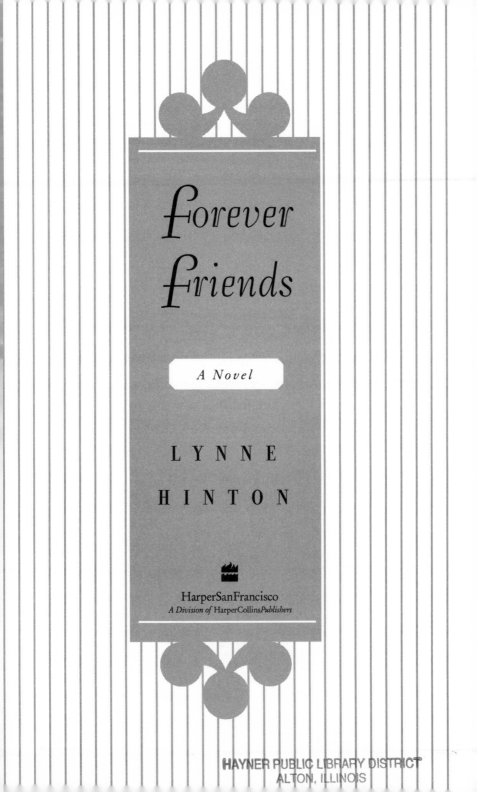

HarperSanFrancisco
A Division of HarperCollins*Publishers*

HarperCollins books may be purchased for educational, business, or sales promotional use. For information please write: Special Markets Department, HarperCollins Publishers, Inc., 10 East 53rd Street, New York, NY 10022.

HarperCollins Web site: http://www.harpercollins.com

HarperCollins®, 📖®, and HarperSanFrancisco™ are trademarks of Harper-Collins Publishers, Inc.

FIRST EDITION

Designed by Jessica Shatan

Library of Congress Cataloging-in-Publication Data has been ordered.
ISBN 0-06-251748-1 (cloth)
ISBN 0-06-251749-X (paperback)

03 04 05 06 07 ❖/RRD 10 9 8 7 6 5 4 3 2 1

For Judy Haughee-Bartlett
and Tina Heck,
and Anna Bess Brown

My forever friends.

I gratefully acknowledge the expertise and assistance of the editorial staff at HarperSanFrancisco, especially Renee Sedliar, Chris Hafner, and Priscilla Stuckey. Thank you for sharing the vision.

Forever Friends

One

* A U N T * D O T ' S * H E L P F U L * H I N T S *

Dear Aunt Dot,

Are there any household uses for old pairs of panty hose? It seems so wasteful just to throw them away when they get runs.

—Runaround Sue

Dear Sue,

Of course you can make use of those old hose. You can cover leafy plants in your garden to eliminate the bug problem, and you can use them in your cleaning kit. Simply ball them up and use them like scouring pads. You'll find they're not nearly as abrasive as most cleansers on the market.

*B*e careful of that desk drawer."

The warning came too late. Charlotte walked right around the corner and into the open bottom drawer and nicked her shin, ripping a large hole in her hose and causing a painful contusion just below her knee.

"Gosh. Sorry about that." The desk sergeant winced at the sight of the young woman's leg. "That desk needs to be put somewhere else." She made a clucking noise with her tongue on the roof of her mouth. "You're the second one to run into it this morning."

Charlotte started to ask why the woman hadn't moved the desk aside herself or, at the very least, taped the gaping drawer shut, but since she was not one to make such bold suggestions, especially to strangers who wore guns and handcuffs on their belts, she simply bent down and calculated the damage.

There was a little blood from the gash, but the worst consequence was the unsightly rip she now had in her stockings. She knew there wasn't any way to hide the tear, and she wished she had followed her instincts when she was getting ready and wore pants instead of this dress and panty hose or, even better, that she had listened to her original inclination, which was not to come in the first place.

She was at the correctional facility in Winston-Salem to visit Peggy DuVaughn's grandson, Lamont, who was in jail on a robbery charge. Peggy asked Charlotte to go because she was concerned about his safety and well-being and because she had heard that ministers had unlimited opportunities to see inmates, whereas family members had strict rules about their visitations.

"It's different this time," the older woman said to her pastor after she finally confessed what it was that was troubling her. "He's really going to do better. I know it."

Charlotte had assumed when her parishioner called and asked if she could drop by and talk that she was concerned about her husband, Vastine. His doctor had given him a terminal diagnosis of congestive heart failure and he had only recently become a hospice patient. But the older woman had come into the office and fidgeted and changed the subject from first one thing and then another until Charlotte finally asked what she was doing there. Peggy broke down and told her about her youngest daughter's son, who had gotten mixed up with the wrong crowd in junior high school and had never gotten away from it.

"It's those drugs," she said as if she knew for sure the cause of his downfall. "They get hooked on that stuff and then there's just no way to save them." She tugged at the back of her collar and dropped her hands in her lap. "It's the devil's work," she added with a pained expression.

Charlotte nodded in sympathy with a passing thought of Serena, remembering her own hopes for a family member's recovery.

"Vastine and I tried to keep him, you know, when he was little. Sherry was going through the divorce then and just had so much on her." The older woman's face was pinched and crossed in worry. "We kept him for almost three years."

Charlotte had not heard this part of the DuVaughn family history.

"He was such a sweet boy." Peggy rubbed her hands together. "He and Vastine were real close." Then she paused, looking up. "We never had boys."

Charlotte listened. She knew there were three daughters, Sherry, Bernice, and Madison. They had all attended the church at one time or another. Madison's oldest child had been confirmed at Hope Springs. Charlotte thought she was at college out of state somewhere.

"Little Lamont was a handful, but we were doing the best we could." She stopped. "We got him enrolled in the kindergarten at the school. We put him in Scouts and baseball."

She sat quietly for a few moments.

"We would have kept him, you know." Then she sighed with the sound of regret. "But he got to be too much for us." Peggy shifted from side to side in her chair. "So Sherry took him back and they moved down to Lexington." Her movement in the chair stopped. "And then things just got worse."

The pastor handed Peggy a tissue. She took it and wiped her eyes.

"It's always been little things before now, mostly just boy stuff. I mean, I knew he was heading in the wrong direction, but I kept thinking he'd grow out of it, mature." She paused. "It was stealing this time," she confessed. "He broke into a convenience store. Tried to get into the cash drawer but was only able to take some merchandise. When they caught him," she hesitated and shook her head, "he had a gun."

The older woman wiped her eyes again. "It's serious." She peered up at Charlotte. "He's in the adult unit. They say he threatened the police officer." She dropped her head. "He's definitely going to prison. I saw him when he first got there. He was so scared he cried." Peggy spoke softly. "It just about broke my heart."

Charlotte went around her desk and knelt down in front of her parishioner.

"Sherry won't have anything to do with him, says she's through, told me not to waste my time trying to help him."

The pastor reached up and placed her hand on Peggy's shoulder.

"But how can a mother, a grandmother, let one of her babies stay in a place like that and not visit, not try to get him out? He was so scared," she said again as she reached in her purse for another tissue and held it in her hands.

Charlotte nodded, a gesture of sympathy, but she still did not speak.

The older woman looked down at the young minister kneeling in front of her. "I can only visit on Friday nights, for just fifteen minutes," she said, leading up to the request. "But I was thinking that maybe you could go, say you're his pastor." Peggy hesitated. "Maybe you can check on him today or tomorrow." She seemed embarrassed. "If you could just go and make sure he's okay."

Charlotte wasn't sure what to say. She had never gone to a jail before, and the sudden request from her church member was disconcerting.

"Peggy," the minister replied sincerely, "I'm not sure they'll let me see him."

The older woman nodded submissively. "I understand. You don't even know him. And it is a big thing to ask of you to go all the way over there."

Charlotte rolled back to rest on her heels and read the woman's face. Peggy DuVaughn was quiet but strong. She wasn't really a leader in the church, not very active or out-spoken, but watching her as she sat in the pastor's office, so broken and vulnerable, Charlotte thought of who she had been in the church. She considered all the years that Peggy had been caring for her husband, years without complaint or request, years of displayed gratitude for her church's support and her pastor's visits.

Peggy always thanked Charlotte for her prayers, even wrote her notes from time to time to tell her how much the sermons on tape had meant to the two of them when they were unable to attend the worship services, how appreciative they both were for her care during her husband's more criti-cal times.

Charlotte focused on the older woman, thinking that she had believed that Peggy's only problem had been Vastine's health, that this was all she thought about or dealt with or worried over. The pastor felt surprised and sad to learn that Peggy had been troubled for so long about her grandson and that she had never felt free enough to say anything to her pastor or to anyone else in the church.

The burden of shame for this woman, she thought to herself, is as serious as Vastine's heart condition. This disappointment and regret, this dysfunction of her family, has broken her and chained her spirit even more than her husband's terminal illness. Peggy DuVaughn had borne the weight of her grandson's addiction and troubles in silence, as if his choices, his mistakes, were a reflection of her years of care or lack of care, depending on which situation she felt more guilty about.

"Of course I'll try," Charlotte said to Peggy. "I'll call the chaplain this afternoon and see if they'll let me see him."

And that had been it. With that promise made to her parishioner less than twenty-four hours earlier, she had visited Margaret to tell her that she was not able to go with her and the other friends to her doctor's appointment, and she was now standing in the Forsyth County Jail, her panty hose ruined, her leg cut and bleeding, and she was about to go behind guarded and locked doors to visit an armed thief she had never laid eyes on.

"You'll need to leave your purse in one of those."

The desk sergeant pointed to the lockers on the wall to their right. "It's fifty cents," she added.

Charlotte pulled out her wallet and took out two quarters. She walked over and placed the change in the slots and opened the locker. She put her purse inside, remembering that she had already given her driver's license to another police officer and hoping that she wouldn't forget it. She shut the door and pulled out the key. She walked back to the sergeant.

"Okay, just stand there and they'll open that door for you. Then you'll be in a waiting cell and they'll open the next set of doors. Then you turn to the left, and the visiting booths will be right in front of you. A guard will send the prisoner to you in a few minutes. Just wait until he comes."

Then the sergeant left Charlotte standing in front of a large steel door before the minister was able to ask the woman to repeat the instructions.

Suddenly, the large door in front of her opened, and she heard a voice on the intercom telling her to step inside. When she did, the door shut hard behind her. A few seconds passed, and another door in front slid open with a loud clang. She stepped through the doorway and it closed. She scanned the area to her right and then to her left, noticing a hallway with a set of doors. She moved in that direction, aware that she was being watched, and opened one of the doors in front of her. It was a small chamber with a stool in front of a large glass window, a telephone receiver hanging on the right.

She walked in as the door shut behind her and sat down on the stool, wondering if someone was still observing her.

Through the window before her, Charlotte was able to see to the other side, where there was a narrow hallway. Several inmates walked past in bright orange coveralls. A couple of them stared at her as they passed by. She tried to appear unalarmed and unafraid as she sat waiting for her visit to begin. There were sounds of men laughing and doors opening and closing; it seemed that at least fifteen minutes had passed since she had been inside the booth.

She was just about to go out and ask for assistance when,

finally, she heard a door on the other side of the booth open. Two men, one a guard, the other an inmate, walked by her, passing without any attention, and then turned around and walked back. They stood directly in front of her.

"Lamont?" she asked but wasn't sure they could hear her. Then the young man in the orange suit nodded.

The guard stared suspiciously at the female visitor and then spoke to the young man. "You got twenty minutes with your pastor," he said sharply and then turned to Charlotte as if he questioned her professional standing.

Lamont sat down on the stool on the other side of the window.

"Can you hear me or do we need to use these?" She picked up the telephone receiver.

"No," he shook his head. "I can hear you all right."

The woman nodded. "I'm Charlotte Stewart," she said as an introduction. "I'm your grandparents' pastor."

He didn't respond.

"In Hope Springs," she continued.

He nodded but didn't speak.

"Your grandmother Peggy asked me to visit."

He nodded again.

"She was worried about you."

Still no response.

He was bigger than she had expected him to be, broad across the shoulders and built like a football player. Charlotte had not really known how he would look since Peggy had only shown her pictures of him when he was a little boy. And since she knew he had been on drugs a long time, she had just assumed he would be skinny, frail, poorly in appearance.

His size and healthy presence surprised the young pastor, and she realized how the demeanor of addicts can be deceiving. Even until the last days of Serena's life she had shown none of the usual signs of addiction. She wasn't gray or wiry or used up. Just the opposite. She seemed like the girl next door, strong, vibrant, alive. She had fooled everyone, especially her own sister, into thinking that she didn't have a problem.

Charlotte scanned the young man before her and wondered how long it had taken for his family to accept that he was addicted—how many lies they had heard, how many cover-ups of disappearances and stories of why he needed money they had sat through. She wondered at what point he had started stealing from them, first just a few dollars from his mother's wallet, then jewelry and small items, and then finally scheming robberies. Serena hadn't gone that far, but Charlotte certainly knew the stories of the people her sister had associated with.

"Granddaddy okay?" Finally the young man spoke.

This time it was Charlotte who nodded.

The young man seemed unsure of what to say next.

"Nothing's wrong with Granny Peg, is it?"

Then Charlotte realized he was trying to figure out why she had come.

"No," she answered reassuringly. "Everybody's okay." Then she set her arms on the steel counter in front of her.

"I'm here because your grandmother asked me to come see you."

He relaxed a bit and nodded again as if he understood.

She saw the fear in his eyes then, the slight edge of worry that kept him jerking behind and around him every time he heard a noise. She didn't know if he was only jumpy because of being in jail or if he was still coming off something.

"How long have you been in here?" Charlotte asked.

"Three weeks," he answered.

She figured that he would have gotten any drugs out of his system by then. His restlessness was from being in the jail. His grandmother's suspicions were right.

"And do you know when they'll post bond?"

He shook his head and swiveled around. A door slammed behind him.

"Don't matter anyway," he responded. "Mama said she won't pay anymore and she won't let Granny give me any money."

Charlotte nodded. "And your dad?" she asked, not knowing any of the circumstances surrounding Sherry's divorce or of the relationship Lamont might have with his father.

He just shook his head.

The absent father, Charlotte thought. Throughout the entire time that Serena had been in trouble, their dad was nowhere in the picture. The first time, more than ten years ago, when she had called to ask for help for her sister, he told her that he didn't know what he could offer in terms of assistance since the money was tight in their house and he was unable to return to North Carolina. When she had asked about them coming to Texas, he said he didn't think it was a good idea for them to stay with him.

That was the only time Charlotte had spoken to him about Serena's addiction and the problems in their household. That was the only time she had asked for his help.

"Have you seen your lawyer?"

"Right after it happened," he answered. "But I don't know nothing."

Charlotte thought about asking about the charges but decided it wouldn't mean anything to her anyway. Besides, she told herself, I'm not an attorney; I'm a pastor. I should stick to my own duties.

"You scared?" she asked, modeling Marion, her therapist, who always got right to the point.

He shook his head and sat back on his stool as if the question offended him.

"Your grandmother seems to think you might be scared since this is your first time in an adult unit."

The young man spun around nervously as if he were concerned that someone might have heard what his visitor just said.

Charlotte leaned on her elbows.

"Look, I know this is awkward. Peggy, your grandmother, just wanted me to see about you." Charlotte slid her fingers together. "She said you were upset when you got arrested, that you've never been in an adult facility before and that it shook you up pretty bad." She sat forward on the stool. "I just came to check on things."

The young man eased a bit and nodded again at the young woman. "I'm all right now," he answered. "Tell her I'm fine."

"Okay," Charlotte responded. Then there was a pause in the conversation.

"Is there anything I can get for you?"

He shook his head.

Charlotte checked her watch, unsure of what to ask next. The steel door that she had come in opened and slammed shut, and the pastor flinched.

"You scared being here?" Lamont leaned in toward Charlotte.

She felt it was a fair question. "Yeah," she replied. "I thought it was pretty unsettling coming here."

She sat back. "I've never been in a jail," she confessed. Then she continued. "I think it's cold and loud. And frankly," she added, "all these people with guns make me jumpy."

"Yeah, in Juvie, only a couple of the guards had guns," Lamont replied, his face softening.

He had given her something with that exchange, and Charlotte decided not to push for anything extra at that moment.

The young man stared at her as if he had more to say, but then he was startled by an announcement made on the PA system overhead.

There was an awkward pause, and Charlotte seemed unsure of what else to ask. She decided to focus on simple questions.

"How's the food here?"

"It's all right." Lamont shifted on the stool. "They have a canteen where you can buy stuff."

"They let you keep your money?" she asked.

"Nah, I ain't got no money." Then he dropped his head. "One of the other guys who's been here awhile, he gives me some of his food. He don't eat too much."

Charlotte studied the young man, handcuffed and dressed in the county jail worksuit. She had seen the bruises on his wrists when he first sat down. As his frightened eyes darted from side to side and his chest rose and fell in shallow breaths, Charlotte thought about freedom. She considered living unchained and unobserved, being permitted to walk without restraint and make her own choices about where to go next and how long she could take to depart and arrive.

She thought how afraid the young man must have been, locked and vulnerable in a cell with potentially dangerous men. She wondered what had been taken from him and what he had lost. What were the consequences of his mistakes? And even though Charlotte wasn't sure she really liked the teenager, and even though she believed that what Lamont was learning in jail was necessary for him to break out of his addiction and criminal behavior, she was still sympathetic as she watched the young man through the glass.

He started to bounce his right leg in a sort of nervous way, his entire body shaking from the effect, and she figured she needed to talk about something. She thought that perhaps the silence was making him feel more disconcerted. She considered talking about his grandparents, but before she could give any information or ask any questions, the guard who had brought Lamont came up behind him and yelled, "Time's up!"

Lamont quickly rose to his feet and offered only a brief nod toward the pastor as a means of good-bye.

"I'll see you later," Charlotte replied as he started walking away. The abruptness of his departure left her feeling disoriented and unaware of what she needed to do to leave her booth.

She sat on the stool for a few minutes trying to remember the way out, consoling herself that the visit hadn't been a complete failure. Finally, she recalled the hallway, the large steel door to her right, and the holding cell, the direction from which she had come. She got up from her stool and walked out of the small chamber. When she got to the first door of the holding cell, it suddenly opened in front of her. She walked in, it closed, and the next door opened. She headed out, retrieved her purse from the locker, went to the first police officer she had met, picked up her license, handed in her visitor's badge, and walked out the front door.

She stood outside and breathed deeply. It was a satisfying winter afternoon, cold without too much wind, bright sunshine, crisp, fresh air. *It's a clean day,* her mom would sometimes say when Charlotte and Serena would get home from school and sit with her on the porch.

On those days her mom wasn't wearing a lot of makeup or flashy jewelry. Her clothes were neat and ironed. She'd smile and ask them how things were at school. She'd brush their hair or hand them pieces of sour candy, pieces of gum, or long, narrow chords of licorice. Serena would show her the pictures she had drawn in class, and Charlotte would get as close to her mother as she could. She'd seem calm and interested and normal, and Charlotte was sure things had changed.

A clean day, she would say, and the little girl thought it meant the longed-for break in time when everybody got to start over, when everything wrong was made right, a brief reprieve from reality when all that was cluttered and broken and strewn about was picked up, fixed, and set aside, a day of redemption finally signaling a change.

It was what her mother had truly desired and what Charlotte had never really found. Joyce could make it seem real for a while, make it appear as if it were really happening, but then Charlotte would hear the clinking of bottles in a bag, see the light in the kitchen burning after midnight, and she learned that a clean day was just something intended about the weather, the angle of the sun on a chilly day, a wish that within a few hours had faded like a winter day into a cold, dark night.

Charlotte stood at the entryway of the county jail, breathing in the memory of her mother's words and the realization of her freedom. She stood, considering in the vastness of the outside and the permission that was hers to come and go anywhere she wanted.

She walked to her car thinking about Lamont, about his family and their sorrow. It could just as easily have been Serena she was visiting in jail, or it even could have been she herself who had turned to drugs. She wondered if it was grace that had saved her from that life and why her sister or Lamont hadn't been granted the same portion.

Lifting her face, she felt the gentle winter breeze stirring in her hair, the strength of the midday sun warming her neck and shoulders. She folded her hands together, and without knowing what words to say, she said a brief prayer for the young boy she had just met. She prayed for the healing of his heart, God's protection and mercy, and the opportunity she hoped for him one day soon to rediscover the opportunity, the gift of freedom. She prayed for Peggy and Vastine and Sherry, all of whom carried and wrestled with the weight of Lamont's misery. She prayed that all of them, including herself, might one day be completely free.

The young woman opened her eyes and took in the air that was hers to enjoy. She unlocked her car door, stood for a moment, and then turned the key, relocking the door. She was disappointed that she had missed the doctor's appointment with Margaret, and now it was too late to join the women for lunch in Greensboro. She thought for a moment and decided that she might as well get something to eat there.

She buttoned her coat and threw her scarf around her, and except for the large area on the inside of her leg where her panty hose were ripped and exposed, Charlotte felt warm and content.

Seeing a sign for a coffee shop, she headed in that direction without seeing Dick Witherspoon and his sister-in-law as they hurried out of the office across the street and got into his car.

Two

*AUNT*DOT'S*HELPFUL*HINTS*

Dear Aunt Dot,

I have heard that bloodstains on clothes should be washed in hot water, but that doesn't seem right to me. What do you say?

Red-Blooded Woman

Dear Red,

You're correct not to feel good about that advice. Blood tends to set in warm water. It's best to soak the clothes in cold water and then treat the area with a stain remover; or try hydrogen peroxide on the unsightly spot. Or, best, try a little salt on the fresh stain. And remember, the quicker you can work on cleaning bloodstains, the better chance you have for a complete removal!

*M*argaret, your mammogram is clear; the results from your blood tests are great; the CAT scan didn't show anything abnormal."

The doctor pulled the chart away from his face and studied his patient. "Of course, it does appear that you may have a spot."

Margaret's heart sank. She held her breath, fixing her eyes on the man's lips as she waited for the words she thought would be heavy enough finally to break her fragile heart.

"On your sleeve." He pointed to the inside of her elbow where some blood had soaked through onto her blouse.

Margaret glanced down and saw the stain. She looked back at her doctor with an expression of indifference and a bit of contempt that he would joke at such a time.

He immediately realized the weight of her anticipation, cleared his throat, and concluded his remarks. "I'm sorry. Let me go on." He smiled reassuringly. "The tests are all normal. You're in great shape, Margaret, cancer free."

The woman exhaled. She bowed her head and whispered, "Thank you," a quiet prayer of gratitude, and then opened her eyes. She nodded in approval at her physician and sat quietly, letting his words float above her, waiting until they drifted down upon her and soaked into every fiber of her being.

"Normal tests. Cancer free." The words washed over her like rain, clean, perfect rain.

It had been just over a year since the diagnosis, twelve

months, two weeks, and four days since the first mention of this offensive and malevolent clump of cells that grew within her breast tissue and threatened her foundation of life. Twelve months, two weeks, and four days of procedures and tests and waiting to see. Twelve months, two weeks, and four days of uncertainty and fear and sleepless nights and dogging ideas of demise. And Margaret hoped but wasn't sure that the rain of her doctor's words was enough to ease the year of emotional and spiritual drought.

It had been for more than four complete seasons that she had been living a pretense while entertaining anxiety that nobody, not her siblings and family members, not her doctor, not even her closest friends, could possibly understand. As hard as she tried not to do so, for more than a year she had been preparing herself for the worst while trying to appear as if she believed the best.

Margaret was sure she had fooled everyone into thinking she was strong and equipped and prepared to handle any treatment, any further surgery, any bad news. No one else, she thought, saw the lag in her thinking or the dulling of her purpose. No one else knew of the colorless way she now dreamed and she believed that she had managed to hold all of her trouble inside. But in spite of what she hid from others, in spite of how she thought she appeared, the truth was, in the past twelve months, two weeks, and four days, Margaret had lost her edge.

She did not know for sure the exact moment it had happened. There was not one day when she felt it loosen and slip away, an hour when she watched it narrow and disappear. It had been like a sand dune on the beach, sifting and sieved; it was simply there one summer and gone the next.

She had talked openly regarding her concern, potential metastasis and a recurrence. She had gone to the library, read medical reference guides and stories of healing. She had learned how to access the Internet and find the latest information about breast cancer. She had asked questions of her physicians. She'd read reports and even gone to a medical conference. She had spoken of what might happen if the tumor spread. She'd done everything she thought she should do to be defensive and healthy and prepared, but none of the education or information or resolution could stop the simple and gradual way she had come undone.

Over time and without evidence, Margaret had convinced herself that the cancer had returned, had sneaked through bloodlines and brain waves, and was growing all over her body.

As hard as she had tried to maintain a rationality in her thinking, a levelheadedness during the time right after her surgery, as diligently as she had tried to pretend that nothing was wrong, there were moments when she thought she literally felt her cells bump and divide, moments when she was sure she heard tumors bud and flower across organs, moments when she was drowned in the perception that she was riddled with the disease and was taking her last breath.

And it was in these moments, these dark and petrifying moments, that Margaret readied herself for death. And no one, not Jessie or Charlotte or Louise or Beatrice, no one had been with her; no one had struggled alongside her; no one had stood ground with her when she wrestled and was finally overcome by the terror. This she'd had to do alone.

So that now, even as she sat in her physician's office hearing the words she was convinced she would never hear, seeing the proof on paper, the clear evidence that nothing abnormal was growing inside her, Margaret realized how deeply those moments of terror had eaten away at her confidence and eroded her sense of peace. And she was not sure she would ever be able to recover what had already been lost.

It would take a lot of time, she thought as she sat across from her doctor, to eradicate the damage of doubt, months, maybe years to tighten up what had been stretched and pulled loose, a lifetime perhaps to patch up what was threadbare and unattached. And yet maybe, Margaret prayed in her fleeting and hopeful thoughts, maybe I can now finally be free.

She waited in the wake of the good news, trying to imagine herself healed, trying to think how it would be not to take note of every change in her body, but she knew that even with the positive prognosis proven and displayed, it remained difficult to hold such confidence, to keep it in her mind.

"I am so grateful, Dr. Morgan. I couldn't have made this journey without you," she said, laying her hands across her lap, trying to be pleased. "You have been extraordinary."

The physician smiled. "It is always a pleasure to deliver favorable results." He picked up her chart again, checking over the reports.

"I don't think you need to come back for a year." He flipped the pages one after the other. "Mrs. Peele, I am officially releasing you until your next annual physical exam." And he wrote a note in the chart and closed it.

"And, Margaret," he peered at her intently, "try not to worry about things anymore."

His patient stood up. It startled her that he had noticed her anxiety, and she wondered if he had in fact discovered it or if this was what he said to every patient he dismissed. She nodded, without question, and tried to begin to honor his advice.

"I will do my best," she responded, feeling a forgotten lightness in her chest. And suddenly the silence between them became awkward.

"Well, nothing personal, Dr. Morgan, but I'm really glad that I don't have to see you any time soon."

He pushed his chair away from the desk and walked around to where Margaret was standing. He held out his hand. "It is not taken personally."

The woman reached for his hand and then wrapped her arms around him in a hug. She pulled away, astonishing even herself, and then retreated. "Thank you again," she said, a bit embarrassed.

"You're welcome." And he headed over and opened the door. "Stop by the nurses' station and ask them for a little peroxide to get out that stain." He pointed to her arm.

She noticed the spot on her blouse again.

Then he asked, "So, what will you do now?"

The older woman moved toward the door. "I'm not sure," she replied. "Maybe I'll take up tap dancing or roller skating." She did not mention trying to mend the hole in her heart, sewing together the fraying strings of her faith, or recovering the loss of peace. She did not ask what he suggested for such intensive repair.

"Well, just make sure you wear knee and elbow pads," he answered. "For the skating," he added. "I don't guess the dancing could be dangerous."

She waved and faced the hallway. "At my age, doctor, anything could be dangerous." Then she paid her bill and walked toward the main office, forgetting all about the bloodstain.

Louise, Jessie, and Beatrice were sitting in the first row of chairs, reading books and turning pages in magazines. Margaret watched them for a few minutes, imagining their reactions; and she stood at a distance, just savoring the thought of telling them.

She loved looking at these women, her three best friends. Louise, square and broad and always acting tough, a woman's woman with the heart of a child. Jessie, tall with wide sweeping arms that reached around any hurt thing. A smile that could not be contained. And Beatrice, short and round, her smooth hands and blue eyes always busy to temper sorrow. Margaret loved seeing them there, knowing they were waiting for her, hoping for good news. She studied them, the familiarity of their faces, the short hairstyles, still a reminder of what they had given to her when they'd shaved their heads after her surgery. She stood at the door and re-membered how fortunate she was to have such women in her life. Forever friends, they called themselves, because they knew what they had would last.

Earlier in the month, when she first knew about the ap-pointment, she had told the women that it wasn't necessary for them to come with her, that she was fine to go to this visit alone. But Jessie had shaken her head, waving her off, Louise had spat out some obscenity, and Beatrice had simply pre-tended not to hear. Even Charlotte had written it on her calendar weeks ahead. None of them would consider it. Nothing was going to change.

In this past year of her life, someone had gone with Mar-garet to every one of her appointments. It had been a com-bined effort on the part of her friends. She hadn't known how it had been put together, who had masterminded the at-tention, but right before every scheduled visit, somebody showed up at her house, ready to drive her into town. Oncol-ogist, surgeon, physical therapist, her regular physician, even the pharmacist—she had not faced an appointment on her own. And they had made it quite clear that they weren't about to miss this last one.

Jessie had changed the date of her departure for Africa, determined that she would not be absent from this event. Even though there was a price adjustment for her airline ticket, she paid the extra money and told James without apology they would be leaving a day later than planned.

Charlotte had come by the day before and, in tears, canceled going with them only because she had been asked to see someone in jail out of town. The only slot available for a visit had been the same time as Margaret's appointment. She promised to try to meet them for lunch or at least stop by the house when she returned to town.

The other women decided that all of them would go with her to see the doctor, promising not to go into the examination room this time but to wait in the reception area. They unanimously agreed that if it was good news they would go out together for lunch. And if it was bad news, well, they'd figure that out when the time came.

Margaret walked into the waiting room, and the three women leaped to their feet, books and magazines falling to the floor.

"Well?" It was Beatrice who asked.

Margaret stood quietly for a minute and then declared, "All clear."

"Well, thank you, Jesus!" Jessie said, throwing her arms up in the air.

Louise placed both hands across her chest and sighed heavily, and then before she knew what had happened Beatrice pulled her into herself and started to jump.

Margaret stood back, laughing.

"Would you please get off me?" Louise pushed the other woman away. "I'm not the one who got the good news! Why don't you jump on her?" She and Jessie stepped away and pointed at Margaret.

Beatrice turned and started to grab her other friend.

Margaret quickly moved aside. "That's all right, Bea," she replied. "Let's just celebrate with lunch." And she hurried toward the door, holding it open for the three women.

Louise and Jessie gathered their things, followed Margaret, and walked through the door, stopping just as they got outside, but Beatrice would not be turned away. She waited in front of Margaret until her friend acquiesced and held open her arms. Beatrice fell into them and, twirling, lifted her off the floor.

"I am so happy!" she said, the tears flowing down her cheeks.

"Yes, Bea, so am I." Margaret relaxed, and Beatrice finally put her down.

They remained at the door while Beatrice took out a tissue to wipe her eyes.

"I have been so worried for so long," she said, blowing her nose. "Lots of people, you know, they find out it's spread to other places," she added. "But I never said anything because I knew this was really hard for you."

Margaret was surprised. "What do you mean, this was hard for me?"

Beatrice returned to the chairs, picked up her coat and purse and Margaret's jacket from the coat tree, put the magazines and books back on the table, and headed out the door. Margaret walked out behind her, taking her jacket and slipping it on.

"Oh, really, Margaret, you don't think anybody bought

that tough-woman routine, do you?" Beatrice put the wet tissue in her pocket. "We all thought this was taking you under."

"Wait, who all thought that?" The two women joined Louise and Jessie in front of the main door.

"Everybody, didn't we?" Beatrice faced the others.

Louise and Jessie were confused.

"We all knew that Margaret was worried about the cancer coming back," Beatrice said, catching them up on what they had missed.

"Scared shitless," Louise answered. "But nobody really knew what to say." She pulled the collar of her coat around her face.

"We prayed a lot," Jessie added.

Margaret stared in disbelief at her friends. "Everybody knew?"

"Yep," Beatrice responded. "Even had a committee meeting about it." And she put on her coat.

"Well, we said that was why we were meeting, but we also checked out the wig shopping on the Internet," Louise added, scratching her scalp.

"I still think I should have bought that Diana Ross one." Jessie fingered a strand of hair.

Margaret shook her head, still surprised that she hadn't fooled anyone into thinking she was doing fine with her diagnosis.

"It's just so good that you're okay." And Beatrice reached over and hugged her again.

"Well," Margaret said hesitantly and with resignation, "I guess I can't keep anything from you women."

"Not even where you hide your liquor." Louise moved next to her friend.

Margaret wasn't sure how she felt, the contents of her heart exposed and studied. Did it offend her or soothe her to find out that what she had held as private pain had been scrutinized and combed through? She had been so sure that her portrayal of tidy and capable disease management had convinced the others that she was okay, that now she felt ambivalent about what had been shared. But she shook aside her thoughts as she lifted her face in the bright afternoon sun, and decided that it wasn't the day to stay distracted by what she didn't know. It was the day to bask in what she knew for sure. The cancer was gone.

Beatrice glanced out into the parking lot. She turned to the other women. "I think we should have lunch somewhere nice."

"That's the general idea of celebrating," Louise replied. Then she faced Jessie, who was standing next to her. "You still got to go?"

"Yes, I'm afraid I've got to take care of some things before we leave in the morning." And then she walked over to Margaret. "But first, tell us exactly what the doctor said."

Margaret pulled her jacket tightly around herself and gave the details of the good news as the four women walked to Beatrice's car. She said the words slowly and deliberately, letting each syllable sound and fall, the answer to their prayers drawn out and enjoyed.

She told them about the blood tests, the CAT scan, and the mammogram, all the information that had been delivered and placed inside her folder. She told them of the doctor's comment about the stain on her sleeve and how she had not considered it funny at the time; but now she could even laugh a bit at his attempt to be humorous. She mentioned the hug and the surprised look on his face and even her fear that the news might not be positive. She told it all particularly and with great joy as they strode to where they had parked.

They stopped at the two cars they had driven and turned to face the doctor's office.

"I'm glad we aren't coming back here for a while," Louise said.

"That makes two of us," Margaret responded.

"Yes," Jessie added.

And they waited quietly, thinking how good it felt for Margaret to be done with those monthly visits, those agonizing hours of tests and troubles.

"We're going to miss you, woman." It was Beatrice who broke through the silence to say good-bye to Jessie.

"Yes, we certainly are," Louise said.

"You promise to send postcards, right?" Margaret asked.

"Absolutely. And I'll take lots of pictures," Jessie answered.

"Well, if you touch anybody's ass, do get a shot of that." Louise winked, reminding the women of Beatrice's cruise, when she had goosed the captain of the ship.

"Certainly," Jessie said. "Though I expect that's highly unlikely on this trip." Then she said to Margaret, "I just can't tell you what hearing this news means." She reached out and took Margaret's hands in hers. "You're really okay."

Margaret nodded. "I'm really okay," she repeated, trying to believe.

Jessie hugged her friend and then said good-bye to Louise and Beatrice. They stood beside the other car and waved as Jessie pulled out of the driveway and headed down the road. They waited a bit before speaking.

"Well, how about the steak house?" Beatrice asked.

"No, I don't think I want steak," Margaret answered.

"Chinese?" Beatrice asked as she unlocked the doors and got in.

"No, that food gives me heartburn," Louise responded as she and Margaret climbed into the car.

"Then what?" Beatrice asked as she sat down and fastened her seat belt.

There was a pause as the women thought about a place they could go and eat their lunch.

"Is Charlotte joining us?" Beatrice asked.

"No. She seemed to think she would be busy all morning," Margaret answered.

"Who was it she was seeing again?" Beatrice backed out of the parking space and then stopped.

"She didn't say," reported Margaret. "Somebody in Winston-Salem." Then she added, "I think it's a confidential thing."

Beatrice made a humming noise like she was thinking and glanced over to Louise and back to Margaret as if they might know something she didn't, but one of the women was staring out the window and the other was searching in her purse, neither of them letting on that they knew anything more.

"Let's go to that little diner across the street from the Laundromat where Nadine works." Margaret said this as she placed her receipt in the zippered compartment of her purse and set it on the floor next to her feet.

"That's a wonderful idea," Beatrice added. "They have such good pie. . . . Oh, and I need to give Nadine a check anyway. I forgot to pay her the last time I picked up my cleaning. Will it be all right to stop by there first?"

Since neither woman objected, Beatrice turned the car in the direction of the cleaners, and when they arrived she parked and the three of them went inside.

Margaret stood by the large machines. She smiled. She wasn't sure why, but she always felt pleasure in being in a Laundromat. She thought it had something to do with the clean odors of fabric softener and bleach, the swirl of clothes in the dryer, and the noise, like soft humming. She found it comforting, and when she had heard months before that Nadine had taken a job there she thought it was a good place for the young woman to start over.

"I think it would be nice to work here," she said to Louise as Beatrice went to the front desk to ask if Nadine was in the office.

Margaret and Louise listened to the thumping in the washing machines, the quiet conversation between a young mother and her child. They watched as a man folded his clean clothes.

"I don't know," Louise responded in a sort of whisper, "there's always strange folks in Laundromats." And she looked around, noticing who was there.

"Not strange," Margaret answered as she closed her eyes and breathed in deeply, "just people down on their luck, busted washer or traveling through town. Just people with dirty clothes." She opened her eyes. "I always found the Laundromat to be a place of comfort, a place of camaraderie." She stopped.

Then she glanced down at her arm as if she had remembered something. She quickly changed the subject. "Hey, maybe Nadine will know how to get this out."

Louise wasn't sure what she meant. She shrugged her shoulders. What was Margaret saying? She herself had never felt comforted in a Laundromat. It wasn't a place she wanted to visit. She had never felt camaraderie there. It had never been a place she enjoyed, and it surprised her to hear that Margaret thought so.

Beatrice returned to the two women. "She's not here today." There was a straight line of pink lint on the front of her coat where she had leaned across the counter. "Exams," she added, then she took a breath like a person sniffing a fine glass of wine. "Don't you just love the smells in here?" she asked. "Just like a baby's butt." And she turned toward the door.

Louise looked over at Margaret, who was nodding. She

shook her head at what she didn't understand, and the three women walked out of the Laundromat, across the street, and into the diner. They found a booth and sat down. Beatrice and Louise sat together on the side facing the back of the restaurant. Margaret sat opposite them.

All three reached for the menus, trying to decide whether they would choose the daily special or split a pizza. The waitress came and went a few times before they finally made up their minds.

Margaret sat with her head down and paid no attention to the young couple who came in just after they did and sat down in a booth on the other side of the diner. She did not see it was a familiar face until she had finished her lunch, had engaged in a long discussion about a recipe, and was ordering a cup of coffee with her dessert. Then, just as she snapped up her head to motion to the waitress that Beatrice had made up her mind about which pie she wanted, she noticed that it was Lana Jenkins who lowered her eyes and bit her bottom lip as the man sitting with her reached across the table and touched her on the cheek.

It was such a blatant gesture of familiarity, such a moment of tenderness, that Margaret blushed to have seen something so intimate. She quickly turned away.

"I wish Jessie could have eaten with us," Beatrice said after she placed her dessert order.

"Yeah, she loves the meat loaf," Louise replied, reaching for the sugar. Then she added, "What is it, Margaret? You see somebody you know?"

Louise and Beatrice both started to spin around to see who it was their friend had noticed, but Margaret spoke quickly. "No, it's nothing. I thought maybe I saw Nadine go in across the street."

The women turned around, neither of them having seen the young girl and the stranger with whom she dined.

"You're so right, Lou," Margaret added, trying not to appear as if she had witnessed anything disturbing. "Jessie would have loved this lunch," she said, thinking how awkward it would have been had Jessie been sitting there beside her and seen what she was seeing.

"Well, I hope they have a lovely trip." Beatrice spooned cream into her coffee. "The two of them deserve a little happiness."

Louise agreed. "They've certainly waited long enough."

Margaret peered just over her friends' heads as the young woman flipped her hair and moved about in her seat nervously. The man would occasionally lean across the table as if sharing a secret, but Lana would pull away, a pained expression on her face.

"Is this pecan or walnut?" Beatrice asked the waitress, who had walked over to fill up their coffee cups and hand them the bill.

"Pecan. You ordered pecan pie, right?" the woman asked Beatrice.

Lana was getting ready to leave, their meals barely touched. The man slipped out of his side of the booth first and then held out his hand, which she took and slid out from behind the table. They stood that way briefly until the young woman pulled her hand away and walked out the door. The man smiled, dropped a few dollars on the table, and hurried behind her.

"Well, it tastes like walnut," Beatrice answered the waitress. "It's good, though; got a bourbon taste to it."

Louise rolled her eyes. "That's why it's called bourbon pecan pie, Bea."

"Is that a fact?" she asked, reaching for a menu to read the dessert listing again.

Louise shook her head and then noticed Margaret's attention still being paid to something going on behind her. She studied her but did not speak of it. "You drink a lot of bourbon, do you, Beatrice?"

"No, I do not. I recognize the taste from candies my mother used to make." Beatrice put a tip on the table and reached for the bill. "Are we ready to go?" she asked. "And by the way, this is my treat," she added. "I just got a raise from my generous husband-boss."

"He can still do that," Louise replied, intending to be sarcastic, but neither Beatrice nor Margaret seemed to notice.

"I'm glad we came here. This is a nice place," Beatrice said as she pushed herself out of the booth. "Good pie. I wonder if they make the desserts here or order them from somewhere else." No one responded as they walked over to the cash register. "Maybe they'd like a copy of our cookbook."

Neither woman answered her. Louise scanned the restaurant, trying to find out who Margaret had seen, but she did not recognize anyone there.

"Thank you for the treat, Bea," Margaret said as she reached for a toothpick. "It was the perfect celebration meal!"

Beatrice nodded. "Well, it's certainly a day for celebration, Ms. Cancer-Free Friend." She took the change from the waitress and placed it in her wallet. "Maybe now you can relax a little and enjoy life."

"Yeah, maybe now you won't be so grouchy," Louise added.

"I haven't been grouchy," Margaret replied.

And the two friends faced each other with raised eyebrows.

"Really," Margaret asked, "have I been grouchy?"

Beatrice placed her arm around her. "You've been fine, Margaret. At least you've had a reason for your temperament." And she grinned at Louise.

Louise rolled her eyes while the three of them got their coats and walked out. They stood at the driveway waiting to go across the street, where they had parked, when a black Cadillac pulled out from the lot, turning in front of them. Beatrice glanced up just as the car moved past.

"That's funny," she said as they hurried to her car, "but that looked just like Lana Jenkins in that Cadillac."

When they got to where they had parked, Beatrice

fumbled with her keys. Louise cut her eyes over to Margaret, who said nothing as she watched the black car speed away.

Beatrice finally opened the doors and stared at Margaret as her friend started to step into the car. "Your color is even healthier," she said.

Margaret, distracted by what she had seen, remained hopeful that Beatrice was right. She got in and buckled her seat belt, still waiting for the truth to soak in.

Three

＊ A U N T ＊ D O T ' S ＊ H E L P F U L ＊ H I N T S ＊

Dear Aunt Dot,

Is a clean desk really the sign of a clean mind?

Dirty Mind

Dear Dirty,

I expect so. There's just no excuse for letting things pile up in your workspace. Designate the last fifteen minutes of every day as cleanup time. Organize the papers and folders scattered on your desktop. Return office supplies to their rightful place. Create a filing system that allows you to put aside the things you don't need right away and have the necessary documents at your fingertips for the next day. Cleaning up before you leave will give you a feeling of completion and productivity, and it will create a sense of readiness when you come back in the morning. Remember: It only takes fifteen minutes a day!

I know it's here somewhere." Beatrice walked into the farthest room with Louise following close behind. "Take off your coat and come on in."

They had stopped at Beatrice's house after the celebration lunch because she wanted to give her friend something she had been keeping for months.

It was an article about a woman in Georgia who had planted and landscaped over three acres of shrubbery into a larger-than-life bonsai garden. The woman had turned her home into a retreat center, and the gardens were meant to be a part of the meditative atmosphere. Beatrice had cut it out when she first discovered it, thinking that Louise might like to read about it and even visit there sometime.

"It was from some gardening magazine I found in Charleston," she said as she walked into the room.

She moved over to the desk that was near the center of the room and lifted piles of papers and sorted through stacks of mail. "When Dick and I went." She searched through trays and flipped open notebooks. "Last fall, you remember?"

Louise didn't answer. She stayed at the door, staring at the mess in this unseen room of Beatrice's house. Her coat was in her arms.

"This is your office?" she asked with a disbelieving tone. She scanned the room. "You actually work in here?" she added.

"Yes. I do all my typing and organizing, all my church and

club activities here, even my sewing." And Beatrice pointed to the far side of the room, which was covered with scraps of patterns, pieces of material, and clothes strewn across a metal bar hung in the corner.

Louise was nervous about entering the room. She remained at the door. "This is unbelievable." And she tried to take in everything that was in the room. She had never been in this part of the Witherspoons' house, and it startled her to see such disorganization from somebody who always appeared so orderly.

"It's here somewhere." Beatrice was still sorting.

"You know, if you threw some of this mess away, you could find what you were looking for." Louise stepped over a pile of newspapers and moved into the center of the room.

"Maybe I stuck it in a book."

Louise bent down and rifled through some of the old magazines situated against the desk. "Did you realize these are from the 1980s?"

Beatrice wasn't paying her any attention. "It was an old edition. I took it from a bathroom in a restaurant." She was intent on finding the article. "La Chadiere, or something like that," she said.

"That doesn't sound like any gardening magazine I've ever heard of," Louise replied.

"No, that was the name of the restaurant." Beatrice dropped to her knees and searched under the desk. "French," she added.

Louise nodded. "Right." She put the magazines down on the floor. "Why do you have all this junk?"

Beatrice stopped her search and yelled, "Oh, leave me alone. I hear it all the time. I'm a pack rat. I hang on to things too long. Dick says it constantly."

From her knees she yanked open the top drawer of the desk, frowned, then stuffed the envelopes and receipts down and shut it.

She opened the next one. "I'm just afraid that I'll throw away something I might need one day." She pulled out a stack of papers and flipped through them. "I know I saw this thing only last week."

"It's not important. Just take me home; I've got some things I've got to do." Louise wiped the dust off her hands onto the front of her pants and started to put her coat on.

"No. I came here to find this story for you, and I'm going to find it." Beatrice pulled herself up from her knees and started focusing on the papers on top of the desk.

Louise noticed the piles of brochures and pamphlets, the shelves filled with books and folders, the unsightly mounds of material, shaking her head. "The thing is, Bea, if you don't know where anything is, how do you plan on putting your hands on it when you need it?"

Louise saw the chair that was rolled away from the desk. She moved over to it and emptied it of the box that was on it. Then she sat down and began to twirl around. "You should just get rid of all this. I mean, what you got here is a landfill in your house, a fire hazard." She whirled all the way around in the chair.

"Aha!" Beatrice said as she turned around to face Louise,

who now had her back to her; the chair not having made it all the way around the second time. When Louise turned to the front again, Beatrice was standing before her, holding pages from a magazine in her hand.

"I knew I would find it!" Then she held it out to the other woman. "See, aren't you glad I don't throw things away?" And she lifted up her chest triumphantly, as if she had been vindicated.

Louise took the article from her and began reading. Beatrice shifted her gaze toward the mirror on the wall behind them and began studying her appearance. She was proud.

Since the shave of her head the year before, her hair had grown back thicker and curlier than it had once been. And she liked the way she had ringlets around her ears and brow. She checked out both sides, with pleasure. She needed to lose a few pounds, but for the most part, she was pleased with how she looked.

Louise read a bit and then reported to her friend, "Bea, this isn't bonsai. This is a labyrinth."

Beatrice turned from the mirror to face Louise. "What do you mean?"

"A labyrinth. This woman landscaped a labyrinth."

Beatrice still appeared confused. "It's not pruning shrubs, like you do? That Japanese thing?"

Louise rolled her eyes. "No. This is a path. In the woods. Trees and long grasses. This doesn't have anything to do with bonsai." She stood up and slapped the papers on the desk.

"What are you talking about? A labyrinth?" Beatrice reached for the article to see for herself. "What is that?"

"It's a path, something you walk around until you reach a certain point, in the middle."

"Well, what would somebody turn their yard into something like that for?" she asked, trying to read over the other woman's shoulder.

Louise picked up the article again and handed her the magazine pages. "To center oneself. To walk and meditate."

Beatrice flipped through the pages, scanning the information as if she had not seen it before.

"Seems like it would make a person crazy to me. Walking around and around, getting all dizzy and disoriented. How does somebody pray in a maze? I thought this was about somebody who made a nice garden for people to visit." Then she pulled open the drawer and placed the pages inside.

"Now, why on earth would you stick that back in there?" Louise sat watching in amazement.

"Oh, you're right." And Beatrice pulled the article out and set it on the stack of magazines next to the trash can. "I keep stuff I'm not interested in down here."

Louise started to say something about the absurdity of this kind of housekeeping, but the phone rang before she could speak her mind.

Beatrice walked around the desk and picked up the receiver. Several papers fell off the desk, but she didn't notice.

"It's Dick," Beatrice said.

"Tell him hey," Louise said.

"Lou says hey." And then, "He says hey back."

There was talk of Margaret and her report, details about the lunch, what they were doing, and what Louise had said about her office. Then Louise quit paying attention. While her friend talked, Louise reached beside the desk and picked up the article she had started reading. She sat down again.

She was intrigued by the Georgia woman's work to clear a patch of woods behind her house and create this large garden, this retreat site. Why would Beatrice have thought she would be interested in the story? She read while the other woman talked to her husband.

"How long will you be gone?" Beatrice asked.

Louise kept reading.

"Well, will you be home for dinner?" Beatrice inquired while she pushed at the sides of her hair.

There was a pause while he answered. Louise stopped and glanced up at her friend.

"Okay, then," Beatrice said after a long while and hung up the phone.

There was silence as Beatrice began haphazardly straightening the magazines on the desk.

"You ready to go?" Louise asked.

"Oh, yeah, I have to take you home." And Beatrice stood away from the desk, staring at the phone.

"Bea," Louise called out, "you okay?"

Beatrice nodded silently.

"What was the phone call about?" Louise folded the article and stuck it in her pants pocket.

"Hmm?" Beatrice asked as if she hadn't heard.

"The phone call. It seems like it upset you."

Beatrice kept picking up magazines and flipping through them.

"Bea!" Louise said sharply. "What's wrong? Is something the matter with Dick?"

The other woman turned away from the desk and stared at the mirror. "No, he's fine," she replied.

Louise waited for her to explain.

Beatrice realized that she would have to tell more of the story. She examined herself, thinking she was now a little flushed, and answered. "It's his brother or his brother's wife. I don't know which." Then she straightened her blouse and smoothed down her skirt with the palms of her hands. "They live near Winston-Salem."

Louise didn't know Dick's family, but she thought she remembered hearing about a sibling who lived somewhere close by. When Bea and Dick had started dating, Bea had thought it was his sister who lived close by, learning only after their wedding that the woman was Dick's sister-in-law. His brother, Louise thought she had heard, had recently been placed in a nursing home.

"Is he all right?" Louise asked.

"Oh, sure," Beatrice responded. "Did you decide you wanted to keep that article?" She'd noticed her friend reading it while she was on the phone.

"Yeah. I'm doing a paper on Georgian labyrinths." It was meant to be a joke.

Beatrice nodded without laughing. Her brow was crossed as if she was worried, and Louise couldn't tell if she was confused by what she had just said or if she was still troubled by the phone conversation.

"Bea, what's the matter? What's the thing with Dick and his brother?"

Beatrice turned to face Louise, who was still sitting in the chair away from the desk. She could see her friend's concern.

"I don't know." She began picking up papers from the floor. Then she added, "There's some story." Louise waited for more. "Some secret he won't talk to me about." Beatrice fixed her eyes beyond her friend. "Something that the brother did or his sister-in-law is doing. I don't know."

Beatrice tapped the papers on the desk to square them up. "He goes up there all the time and comes home all torn up, and he won't talk about it." She set the papers down. "He says his brother is getting worse and that's all that I need to know." She lowered her head. "But I know something else is going on."

She raised her eyes to Louise. "I know he's always been close to Jean, but I don't understand what's happened that he can't tell me. After all, I'm his wife." And then, as if she were embarrassed to say it, "What could be so bad that he can't talk about it to me?"

Louise said nothing as she thought about all the secrets a person holds, all the things somebody says and does not say, the clues in a marriage or in a friendship that point to topics open for discussion and those that are sealed.

She thought about Roxie and wondered if she had ever talked to her husband about her suspicions of her best friend, about the night Louise had gotten drunk and kissed her, then run out of the boardinghouse, staying away for a week, how they had never spoken of the event.

She thought about her own secrets, her own hidden memories. She thought about her mother and the odd way she acted around certain men in the family, guarded and keen-eyed, the relatives Louise was not permitted to visit.

She recalled the stories she had heard from the other women in the mill, stories marked with large chunks of time that were not discussed or reportedly not remembered, stories of lives that appeared to have started at the age of eighteen, lives without childhoods or parents or memories. Lives with so many things not said that it was easier to pretend they never happened than it was to uncover them.

"Everybody's got secrets, Bea," she said softly.

"I don't have secrets," she replied. "I've never had secrets!" She walked away from the desk and sat down in the chair in the corner near the sewing area.

"Then consider yourself fortunate," Louise responded. "They usually aren't something you're glad to have."

Beatrice faced Louise. "What's your secret?" she asked.

Louise's appearance changed. She hesitated a moment, seeming to think about the question, then shifted to face her friend.

"Which secret you want to know about, Bea?" She was forthright, steady.

Beatrice went red and turned away, shaking her head.

"Yeah, I thought not," Louise said.

There was a heavy silence as the weight of what was asked and then taken back settled upon the two women.

"All my life, I've never had a secret." Beatrice rested against the chair. "My family would tell each other things at the dinner table before I got there, and then Daddy would make them hush before I ever heard the joke or the story." She dropped her hands in her lap.

"My sisters and their friends, they used to giggle and talk real low to each other, and I'd try to be a part of the group, try to find out the things they said. The things that made them blush and laugh and seem to come alive, the whispers behind a shield of hands, the silly notes they guarded like they were money or read privately and then tore up into tiny little pieces and scattered them in the fireplace."

She looked away. "Everybody always said I was too young or that I would tell." She stopped briefly, then added thoughtfully, "That I talked too much."

Louise almost laughed out loud to think of Beatrice as a little girl. It was funny to imagine the kind of child she must have been.

"And then I had my own friends, and I'd find out all these things that everybody else knew days or months earlier and that nobody had told me."

Beatrice's bottom lip began to tremble, and Louise suddenly realized the magnitude of what the other woman was telling her.

"I was always the last to know everything, always, always last." Beatrice began to cry. "And then there was Robin and Jenny, like two thieves they were so tight. And I wanted to be more than a mother to them. I wanted to be their friend. But as soon as I would walk into the room where they were or get in the car or sit beside them at the table, they'd just clam up, just quit talking, like I was the enemy or something."

She drew in quick breaths. The tears stood in her eyes and then fell. She reached in her pocket and pulled out a tissue.

"And now this." She dabbed at her eyes. "Now I'm married to a man who has this"—she searched for the right description—"this terrible burden of a secret that he won't tell me." She looked at Louise. "Me, his own wife." She slid her hands down the front of her skirt. "What kind of marriage is it that you can't trust your spouse to tell them this thing that makes you so unhappy, so bothered?" Her voice was stretched, yearning. "Or is it me?" She dropped her face in her hands. "Is it that I'm such a terrible person that nobody trusts me enough to tell me anything?"

And with that it was as if her heart burst, as if years, decades, of sorrow poured across the dam, breaking through every confidence, every assurance, every defense she had ever used to make herself believe it hadn't mattered. "Am I really that bad of a person?"

Louise sat still as her friend fell into the pit of her own dirty little secret, her own cave of vulnerability that she had hidden so well and so long that no one could have guessed it lay buried beneath the veil of ease. Beatrice had never appeared to be upset by what she hadn't known. She had only displayed concern when she couldn't fix what she knew. Louise watched in astonishment as her friend emptied out her sorrow. She'd had no idea that this woman, this bothersome, socializing, busybody woman, could be so completely and terribly alone.

Louise did not get up from her seat. She measured every word she wanted to say from this marked distance between them. She waited and then began.

"Beatrice Newgarden Witherspoon, you are one of the finest women I know. You are kind and well intentioned. You are brave and caring and loyal." She stopped.

Beatrice kept her face in her hands, but she was no longer sobbing.

"I don't know why other people haven't told you their secrets. I could not begin to explain the actions of somebody else. I can hardly explain my own actions." She shrugged her shoulders and sighed, but Beatrice was not watching. "Older sisters and daughters I can sort of understand. You were the enemy to your children and a pest to your siblings." She rocked back in her chair without losing the intensity of her concentration on her friend's great concern. "And sometimes when girls are young, they just tell their secrets to whoever happens to be there at the right time. It isn't a matter of trust or who you like more; it's just about convenience, who was there when it happened. Who was at home when you thought to call and tell somebody."

Beatrice lifted her head. Her eyes were red and puffy.

"And I don't know what to say about Dick. Maybe he's worried that this secret will change how you think about him."

Beatrice shook her head, but Louise resumed talking before she could say anything in response.

"Or maybe it's not his secret to tell. Maybe his brother or his sister-in-law begged for his confidence, demanded he not tell anybody. And even though that might feel awful to you, even like betrayal, it isn't. This secret and not telling it isn't about you or your marriage. It's about them." She stopped and then continued. "And you've got to let it be. You've got to be the one who trusts him. He'll tell you when it's the right time for him to tell you."

Beatrice turned away.

"And sometimes, Bea, people don't tell their secrets not because they don't trust somebody or love somebody enough. Sometimes we don't tell our secrets because we're trying to forget them. It's easier just not to say."

Louise finished her speech and watched as Beatrice sat quietly. She was motionless, calm, displaying not even the slightest physical reaction to what her friend had said. She just stayed lowered in her chair, dissolved in her seat like a child in the principal's office.

Louise did not hurry her or ask her if she was okay. She just sat across from her and waited, thinking that a person never really does know the depth or scope or consequences of the secrets another person can hold inside herself. How even the bearer of the secrets herself never fully understands the burden of her what is clasped and cluttered within the chambers of her own heart until what has been inside comes out. Until what was kept in darkness is brought into the light. And once it is seen or heard or spoken, once it is released from its captivity, once the buried truth is unearthed, it is enough to restrain any temperament, arrest any trailing talk, enough to halt the call for explanation or the need for anything more. The telling of one's secrets silences even the confessing tongue.

There was a long and noiseless passing of time before Beatrice moved. She stood up from the corner chair and walked near the mirror so she could see herself more clearly. She picked away the tiny pieces of tissue that were stuck to her eyelids and cheeks. She found her makeup case in her purse and slowly smoothed on some powder and then, using her fingertips, brushed on a little blush. She painted on her lipstick, patted her thin pink lips together, touched up her short brown hair, and studied the line of her profile, the slight angles of nose and chin. Then she turned to Louise to show her how much better she was.

"Thank you," she said and then spun around to face herself again.

"And now," she said with a huge exhalation, "how do you feel about riding in the car with an old crybaby?"

Louise stood up and walked around the desk, knocking over the pile of magazines next to the trash can. She pretended not to notice. "I would be honored."

The two women did not embrace; they just stayed that way, squared off and satisfied, until Louise finally decided that she had one more thing to say. She pulled on her coat and stuck her hands in her pockets.

"By the way, Bea," she said warmly, "it's no secret why you wanted me to have that article."

Beatrice tried to act surprised by the presumptuous remark. "What do you mean, Lou?" she asked.

"'Local Woman Opens Retreat Center for Gay Vacations'?" Louise waited for a reply.

Beatrice reached over and picked up her purse and walked around her friend. Then she waited as Louise moved past her out of the room. Beatrice turned off the lights and followed her down the hall until they both stood at the front door.

"I don't know what you're talking out, Lou. I thought it was just an article about that funny kind of gardening you do." Beatrice opened the door.

"Uh-huh," Louise answered. "And you claim not to know anybody's secret?"

Beatrice put on her coat and wrapped her scarf around her neck. She slipped on her gloves and scanned the house, making sure it was okay to leave. She walked out and pulled the door shut behind her.

The bright afternoon sun surprised her, and she shielded her eyes from the glare with her hands while trying to remember if her sunglasses were in her purse or somewhere in the car. She stopped, thinking. And then suddenly she recalled that she had left them in the console, in the cup holder that wasn't big enough for anything except an aluminum can. She nodded as a positive sign to herself and then faced her friend to answer what had been left undeclared.

"Really, Lou," she said with a certain flavor, "your sexuality is hardly a secret to anybody." And she walked past her friend, who was standing on the porch, down the steps, and around the car without ever cracking a smile.

four

THE PILOT NEWS

* A U N T * D O T ' S * H E L P F U L * H I N T S *

Dear Aunt Dot,
My youngest child got berry stains on her Sunday dress. Any suggestions for how to clean it?

Berry Frustrated Mom

Dear Mom,
Berry and fruit stains are best treated with salt and a sponge. Just use a little salt (1 teaspoon) and a cup and a half of cold water and sponge the area. Then, if the fabric can handle it, pour very hot water over the stain and dab your detergent directly on the trouble spot and wash. This should do the job! And then I would suggest a bib for the baby since Sunday clothes are not meant for eating berries!

O h, Lord, that's going to make a mess!" Jessie was up from the sofa and into the kitchen before Charlotte could say the prayer of thanksgiving, the last part of the communion service, or tell her parishioner that it didn't matter that she had spilled grape juice down the front of her blouse.

They had read from the Gospel of Luke, said a prayer of confession, and eaten the small wafers symbolizing Christ's body. She had just finished saying the final words of institution for the sacrament, "This is my blood shed for you, the blood of the new covenant, and as often as you do so, take and drink and remember me." Then James and Jessie and Charlotte sipped from their cups.

Somehow the pastor had pulled the tiny vessel away from her lips too quickly and the juice dripped down her chin and onto her clothes. At least three spots colored her new light blue cotton blouse. And now that Jessie had left the room so abruptly there was also an awkward lack of completion to this ritual of pastoral care. She set her cup on top of her communion kit and closed her Bible. Just that kind of a day, she thought, and waited for Jessie to return.

The older woman had called her pastor a week before they were to leave for Africa and asked her to bring communion the night before their trip. At first Charlotte was surprised since she had never shared in the religious ritual with somebody going on a vacation. She had given the sacrament to sick people, troubled people, grieving people, but she had never given it to vacationing people. So at first she wasn't sure it was appropriate or exactly how she should pray or what words of institution she should use.

She wasn't sure if she should follow the order of service from her worship book or just make it more informal and ask God for protection and traveling mercies. She didn't know what Jessie was expecting.

But after she hung up the phone and pondered the request and reconsidered what it meant to leave one's home, even if it was only for a trip, offering communion to Jessie and James made perfect sense. After all, Jesus got the idea for doing this when he knew he was going to die, going to leave his friends. It was a sort of "don't forget me when I'm gone" gift, a good-bye memento. So upon her pastoral examination, it seemed quite logical to her that people should receive the bread and wine when they were going away, making a transition. Jessie had come up with a perfect idea.

Charlotte was now even considering offering it to people next summer, an extra service on Sunday afternoons for people heading out for vacations. It might help the church build community and stay connected in a season when people go in so many different directions.

James broke the uncomfortable silence after he wiped his mouth and set his cup on the coffee table. "You know, she's going to make you go in there so she can clean that." Then, remembering Jessie's thoughts about stains on the furniture, he picked up the small cup and placed it on a coaster.

"Here, try this." Jessie rushed back in the room and handed Charlotte a white cloth dipped in salt water. "I think this is what Dorothy said to try on fruit juice. I've never actually used it myself."

Charlotte took the cloth from Jessie and dabbed at the area where the juice had spilled. The solution was cold, and the area around the stains, growing larger and wetter, began to stick to her. She reached one hand up the inside of her blouse and began to rub the cloth across the blotches. Then she pulled her hand out and looked down.

"It really isn't a big deal, Jessie. I have lots of these stains on my clothes." She handed the cloth to the woman standing over her. "One of the drawbacks of my vocation."

"Professional hazard," James added.

Charlotte nodded.

Jessie frowned and thought for a minute about offering to clean the stain herself or trying to get Charlotte to come into the pantry and make a stronger attempt at removing the spot but decided to let her pastor handle it her way. She held out a dry hand towel.

"And what does Dorothy West know about getting out grape juice anyway?" Charlotte settled in her chair. She took the towel and patted the wet area, trying to dry it.

Jessie returned to the kitchen and responded loudly, "Aunt Dot knows about getting out everything."

Charlotte seemed surprised. She quit patting at the stain. "Dorothy West." She stopped. "Dorothy West is Aunt Dot?"

James shrugged his shoulders. His eyebrows lifted in a question mark as if he wasn't sure of the answer.

Jessie walked in and sat down on the sofa before she answered. "Don't tell me you didn't know that." And she picked up James's plastic cup, wiped off the bottom, and then placed it on a napkin she had left on the table.

"No, I didn't know that." Charlotte tried working a bit more on the stain. "Dorothy West is Aunt Dot of Aunt Dot's Helpful Hints?"

"The one and only," Jessie replied.

"My gosh. I never heard that before." She placed the towel across the arm of the chair and shook her head in disbelief. Then she reached up and tightened the lid on the grape juice container that was on the table in front of her. "That column is printed in papers all over the Southeast."

"Yeah, it's become quite popular." Jessie stacked the three communion cups and handed them to Charlotte. "Lana even said a publisher was interested in putting a book together of all of her tips. A sort of Martha Stewart thing."

"Are we finished?" James asked. "I mean with the activity."

Charlotte nodded in affirmation, thinking it was funny that James had called the sacrament she had shared with them "the activity."

She placed the cups in the plastic sleeve and shut the lid on the small leather box. Then as she thought more about Dorothy, she responded with just one word, "Amazing," and sat back in her chair, taking note once again of her soaked blouse, now clinging to her chest. She had a parishioner who was famous. "Do you think people really write those letters, or does somebody make them up?" she asked, having known about the column in the daily newspaper but never actually having read it.

Jessie turned to notice the clock on the desk near the door. It was getting late. "She says she gets letters from people all the time, so I guess they're real." She tried not to focus on the stain on her pastor's blouse. "I can't believe you never knew that she was Aunt Dot."

Charlotte put her chin in her hand, trying to remember if anyone had ever informed her of this; maybe she had just forgotten. But she thought about it and realized that she simply had never been told.

"I can't imagine Beatrice not talking about it." James reclined, putting his arm around his wife's shoulders.

"Well, I think Bea has always been a little jealous of Dorothy's success," Jessie said quietly.

Charlotte wondered if Beatrice had had Aunt Dot in mind when she started "Bea's Botanical Bits" for the garden club newsletter. "When did she start writing?" she asked Jessie.

"Oh, she's been doing that article for years. Somebody she knew at the Greensboro paper asked her to do something about household hints a long time ago. It was supposed to be just a monthly thing about cooking and decorating. And then it eventually turned out to deal mostly with stain removal, cleaning stuff." Jessie wiped the bread crumbs into the dish towel. "And then they wanted her to write more. People began to call the paper and ask for her. So that's when she became known as Aunt Dot. And she started writing her column in a letter-response form. Seems like she just had a knack for that sort of thing."

"Is her stuff accurate? I mean, does salt water really take

out grape juice?" Charlotte glanced down again at the huge damp area on her blouse. The dark spots did appear to be less noticeable.

"I think she's usually right about the things she says." Jessie had once called Dorothy about grease James had tracked into the house. The older woman had told her to sprinkle baking soda on the stain and vacuum it up the next morning. She had done what Dorothy had suggested, and the next day the grease was gone.

Jessie noticed the area where James had walked in from the kitchen that day so long ago. The carpet was old and torn near the edges, but there was no mess.

Charlotte was still trying to figure out how she hadn't heard that Dorothy was the cleaning matron of North Carolina when James cleared his throat. She took it as a hint and changed the subject to the things at hand.

"Well, I'm glad you called me to come and do this." She reached out and touched Jessie on the arm. "I know you'll have a great trip."

Jessie smiled only slightly, as if she was not sure. "I hope so."

James squeezed Jessie's shoulder and turned toward Charlotte, who had noticed the odd reaction from her friend. "She's worried."

"Yeah?" Charlotte looked at Jessie with the question. "About what?"

James answered for her. "About everything." Then he clarified. "Like whether we got enough money or if the plane will drop from the sky, the off chance we might get malaria or attacked by wild animals."

Jessie rolled her eyes at her husband. "I haven't said anything about wild animals." And she playfully pushed against him with her shoulder.

"No, but you have said you're worried that the safari we're planning to go on isn't safe."

Jessie leaned against the sofa and explained to Charlotte. "I've read stories of how these tour guides get people out away from the city and into the jungle and then they mug them and leave them out there." She shook her head.

The preacher was confused. This didn't seem like an issue that would bother Jessie. "Do you have information about the guides you're using?"

"Very reputable," James replied. "The best in Kenya, we've been assured by the travel agent."

"Yeah, but you never know who they could hire." Jessie folded her hands in her lap.

"Then talk to the manager before you go out, find out how long the guide has been with the outfit, make sure you have other people going with you," Charlotte said, thinking of ways to settle Jessie's mind. It surprised her that Jessie needed this kind of reassurance.

"We know all the tourist safety tips. This is the best safari outfit in East Africa. All the rich people use this one." James paused. "Trust me, Jessie has researched this trip like she was planning to start her own travel agency. She's just getting cold feet."

Charlotte sat up and rested her elbows on her knees. She was directly in front of her parishioner. She stared at her, trying to understand the reason for her discontent.

"You're going to have the time of your life," she said. "This is wonderful that you get to go to Africa. You've been dreaming about this, talking about this, for over a year. Everything is taken care of. You know every place you're going, every hotel, every restaurant. You've checked out everything. It'll be great. And now you know that Margaret is fine." She reached out and took Jessie's hands. "It'll be great!" she repeated.

Jessie nodded, trying to act convinced. "Thank you, Charlotte. And it is wonderful news about Margaret." She paused while she held her pastor's hands, remembering Margaret's appointment earlier that day. She appeared to relax. "And thank you for bringing us communion."

She turned to James. "It just makes me feel better knowing I received the sacrament before we left."

"Absolutely," Charlotte said as she stood up. "It was a wonderful suggestion, and I'm glad you thought of it."

Jessie and James got up from their seats, facing Charlotte.

"I'm going to miss you like crazy," Charlotte said sincerely as she hugged Jessie. "Buy lots of souvenirs. And make sure you write."

Then she hugged James. "She'll be fine. Just get her a couple of cocktails on the plane and she'll forget all of her worries."

"That's exactly what I plan to do," he answered and kissed Charlotte on the cheek. "Thanks for coming over."

"You betcha." She took a deep breath and faced Jessie. "Oh," she said, "I have one more thing, a gift for your trip." She bent down next to her chair and picked up her purse and reached inside. She pulled out a small zippered cosmetic case and handed it to Jessie.

"What is it?" Jessie unzipped the top and peered inside the case.

"It's a little travel kit I made for you. It has international stamps, a phone card, some Band-Aids and Dramamine, sewing supplies, a little clothesline, even a stain stick." She glanced down at her blouse. "Maybe I should keep that for myself," she smiled.

Jessie pulled out a piece of folded paper from the kit and turned to Charlotte.

"It's a copy of the friendship recipe from the cookbook."

Jessie's expression softened.

"I don't want you to forget us," Charlotte said. This was her bread and wine sacrament.

"That's highly unlikely," Jessie said nervously as she slipped the paper into the case and zipped it back together. "But I thank you for the sentiment. It's a lovely gift and I will treasure it and use it on the trip."

Charlotte picked her communion case off the table and her purse from the chair.

"Oh, wait, let me get your coat." James moved around the sofa and headed toward the bedroom.

When he was gone Charlotte asked, "Are you all right?"

The older woman shook her head and then turned away. "I just got a bad feeling about something," she said.

The young pastor studied her parishioner, who was also her friend, unsure of what to say about her premonition. This trip meant so much to Jessie; she had planned and saved for so long. She was excited when she and James first decided to go. She had never mentioned any concern up until now, the day before her departure.

It was unlike Jessie to be worried. This anxiety was out of character for the otherwise unwavering and sensible woman. Jessie had always been the kind of person who made her decisions and then followed through, no regrets, no doubts. This hesitation, this possible change of mind, perplexed the young minister, and she wasn't sure how to respond.

"Here, you're going to need this," James said as he returned to the room and stood next to the two women. He held open Charlotte's coat for her to slip on. "Especially with that big wet spot covering the front of you." He elbowed his wife in the side as if she had been the cause for the soiled condition of Charlotte's apparel.

"Yeah, thanks, I knew I'd need it when I left Margaret's earlier." She put on her coat and buttoned the front. "What's the weather like in Kenya now? I know you said it would be warm, but just how warm will it be?"

"Seventy-five degrees yesterday, the paper said." James rubbed his hands together. "T-shirts and shorts, that's what we got packed."

"And umbrellas; it's still rainy season," Jessie added. "But warm. Might be a little cool at nights, but they say it's mostly like the weather in southern California." She stopped. "Of course, I don't know what the weather in southern California is like."

"Well, I'm sure it will be perfect," Charlotte said, thinking of her own desire to travel. "And I know you won't miss this stuff," she added, meaning the winter storm that had blown through North Carolina, bringing with it a mixture of ice and snow.

"No, we picked this time to go so that we could enjoy some summer weather in winter." James headed toward the front door.

"I just hope the plane won't have any problem getting out of Raleigh," Jessie mentioned with a hint of trepidation as she moved around the table and followed Charlotte, who was walking behind James.

"Oh, I'm sure they've gotten everything cleaned off by now. The roads are fine." She turned to Jessie. "And when do Lana and Wallace return from their trip?" Charlotte remembered that they had gone to the mountains for the weekend. They had not been in church for a few Sundays, which was unusual for them. They were the most active young couple in the congregation.

"Tomorrow," Jessie replied. "I hate that I won't be able to see them before we leave." Her voice took on the worried tone again.

"Yeah, I know they'll miss you." Charlotte reached into

her coat pockets, trying to find her gloves. "Can Lana even cook?" she asked innocently.

Jessie laughed. "Yes, she can," she said, her voice with just a bit of sarcasm and sounding a little more relaxed. "And I know I spoil them. I hear it all the time from Janice and Dorothy."

"You want to see the freezer before you leave?" James had his hand on the doorknob but then stepped away with the invitation. "She's made enough food to last those children for three months." He winked at his wife. "She's cooked more in the last two weeks than she's cooked in her whole life!"

Jessie folded her arms across her chest. "Well, I worry they won't get enough to eat. They both work so much, trying to get Wallace through school and draw an income, they don't even have time to enjoy a decent meal."

"I'm sure you take care of their dietary needs just fine, Jessie," Charlotte replied.

"Needs? She makes sure that grandson gets anything he wants. And that baby?" James shook his head. "That baby is going to be fat, and it's going to be her great-grandmother's fault!"

"It's only baby butter and you know it," Jessie said to her husband.

"Baby butter now, but one day it's just going to be fat."

"Okay, that's my cue to leave. No need to start a fight the night before your big trip." Charlotte stepped toward the door, then turned to give Jessie one more hug. Before doing so, she set down her purse and communion kit and whispered in her ear, "Everything's going to be fine. You just got the traveling jitters is all." And she pulled away, gave her a reassuring smile, picked up her things, and walked outside.

"James, take care of her," she said as she passed him.

"Count on it," he answered, turning on the light as the preacher hurried down the front steps.

She waved from her car, and the couple stood and watched until Charlotte had driven out of the driveway. Then James pulled the door shut and turned off the lights.

"Cold out there," he said. And then he asked, "You going to bed now, or do you have more packing to do?"

Jessie rubbed her hands up and down her arms, still standing at the door, distant and worried. She waited and then walked into the den and began picking up the towels and napkins from the coffee table. "I have a few more things to take care of before I'm ready for bed."

James followed her into the kitchen. "You gone through everything on your checklist?"

Jessie smiled, thinking about the twelve-page checklist she had made months ago. Everything was on that list, including doctor appointments, currency exchange ratios, instructions to Lana and Wallace about watering plants and which locks had keys, bills that had to be paid, and notes to herself about things to buy and what luggage to pack.

She had started the list as a sort of joke when the trip was only a dream that the two of them spoke of in whispers as pillow talk, when it was only a fantasy to stretch them beyond themselves and into adventure. Then as the list began to have tasks that could be completed and marked off, the dream began to grow legs and walk around like a creature with its own breath and purpose. And once they completed assignments, like visiting a travel agency and getting passports, they studied the calendar and set a time. Late January of the following year.

When they first decided on the exact departure date, the twenty-fifth, it seemed so far away neither of them really believed it was true, but they highlighted it on their calendars and continued to mark off items from Jessie's list. Buy traveler's checks. Find out about insurance. Decide which cities they would visit. Get the necessary shots. And before they realized it, they were only days away from the trip and they had done everything that needed to be done.

There was no reason not to go to Africa, no cause to postpone their plans, and there was nothing they had not completed in the preparations. They had thought of everything. Everything. But Jessie was still clouded by something she couldn't explain.

For a few days she considered that it was Margaret; but she knew now that her friend was fine. She worried about her children; but they convinced her they could take care of themselves. She thought about international travel and considered that she was just anxious about potential harm; but she had never been an overly cautious person. She prayed about it and wrestled with it; but she just could not decipher the trouble that lay so near the surface of her plans.

In the beginning Jessie had loved the thought of going to Africa, of visiting the land of her ancestors. She treasured the idea of being in a new world, a different world, of traveling to a place she had only seen in pictures. She envisioned herself there, walking along the dirt roads to find a remote village, shopping for carvings or brightly colored scarves in the open-air market in the city, tracking animals across a vast yellow meadow. She enjoyed the idea of sharing this adventure with her husband, the fact that this was something they were doing together. She loved it and was excited about it, but when the excitement settled down, she was also burdened by it, nervous about it, frightened of something she could not name.

From behind her, James reached his arms around his wife's waist. "Do you want to call Wallace at the hotel and talk to him again?"

She shook her head no.

"Do you want to send an e-mail to the travel agent and get more information about the safari?"

She answered again with a shake of her head.

James took a breath and then asked, "Do you want to cancel?"

Jessie turned around in her husband's arms, standing very near to him. Face-to-face, she stared up into his eyes. Deep and earth brown were these eyes that held her so gently. Eyes that could not hide the depth of feeling he had for her. Eyes that could not cover up the condition of his heart.

It was clear now to Jessie that James loved her, clear and

tangible in a way it had never been before, demonstrated in all the things he had done. She became aware of his devotion with each task they marked off her checklist. During months of preparations and chores, she saw it in the way he willingly turned their dream into reality by taking care of details and considering possibilities without ever complaining about how long it was taking just to get ready to go.

His love, his deep and abiding love, was clear from the way he laughed without irritation when she became frustrated at the questions she wanted answered, the problems that had to be solved. His love was proven by the tender way he had rubbed her hip when the malaria vaccination caused a huge knot. It showed in the straw hat he had driven three hours to the beach and three hours back to bring to her so she would have one on the trip; and it spilled out, loose and unfettered, with the extra money he had given to her a week or so ago.

"Trash cash," he called it. "Money to burn at the markets or in souvenir shops." And he handed it to her like it hadn't cost him a thing, and she knew he had given up the thought of buying the new tractor he had wanted just so they could have a little more in their expense budget.

This trip, with its long list of necessary arrangements and costly tasks, with its considerations and decisions that had to be made before they ever stepped aboard a plane, this trip, with its wardrobe and expenses, had already given her the thing for which she had longed the most. Proof. Real and veritable proof. He loved her. He was home to stay. And now with this tiny but undeniable sense of dread or doubt or worry, this thing she could not name or diagnose or put a finger on, she wondered if what had been acquired in the planning for the trip, being convinced of her husband's love, had really been all that she had wanted in the first place. And now maybe the trip itself was not a good idea.

Jessie stared into his brown and loving eyes and answered the question. "No," she said, trying to persuade herself, "I've been waiting for this opportunity my whole life. To travel across the ocean, to visit Africa, to be with you. It's everything for me."

James held his wife tightly against himself.

She closed her eyes, resting upon his chest, trying to make a way to accept it. The plans were made. The tickets were bought. The organizing had been organized. The children would be fine. Everything was as it needed to be.

They were going to Africa. To Kenya. To Nairobi. They were breathing life into the dream. And sometimes, Jessie understood as she stood within her husband's arms, just that, just the act of watching a dream come true, just that and having it happen at her age, could peel away a woman's courage.

Maybe she was fearful only because she had never come this far. Her unsettling notions were merely the wash and release of fragments of fear, of never daring to dream so deeply and never probing the depth and expanse of desire. She was overwhelmed by the love of James and by the capacity to realize a dream. It was enough, she decided as she wrapped her arms around James, to cause her a bit of panic.

"Surely," she spoke to the dark corners of her mind, the low but troubled space in her soul, "surely, that's all this feeling is."

And she took a breath and leaned into her husband, hoping that whatever lay ahead would not diminish what she had only just begun to know.

Five

THE PILOT NEWS

Dear Aunt Dot,
My grandchild got bubble gum on the floor board of our new car. Help!

Chewed Up

Dear Chewed,
Messy, isn't it? Rub a piece of ice on the gum until it hardens and can be lifted up. It may take a while, so be patient. And you might try paper floor mats in your car when you're baby-sitting in the future. Gum and fabric are no good together.

Well, how did she get it in her hair?" Lana was arguing with Wallace as he was hurrying to get ready for the night shift.

"I don't know," her husband answered from their bedroom. "I gave her a piece after her snack, and I thought she threw it away before I put her to bed." He pulled out a shirt from the closet and put it on.

"I can't believe this," Lana said as she saw how much of her daughter's hair was caught in the wad of gum in the back of her head. "I'm going to have to cut just about all of it off."

The little girl was quiet, standing in her crib as her mother tried to pull as much of her hair away from the gum as she could. She was biting on the ear of a stuffed animal.

"Daddy!" she exclaimed and threw down the toy and held open her arms as Wallace walked into the room.

"No, baby, Daddy can't hold you right now." And he studied the mess his wife was trying to clean up. "I didn't know she had it in her mouth when I put her down." He sounded sorry.

Lana blew out a puff of air. "Just take her," she yelled and left the room. She walked into the kitchen for the scissors. When she returned, he had picked the baby up and was holding her.

"Well, turn her around so I can get it out." Lana reached up and began to cut, trying to remove as little of her daughter's hair as possible. It didn't matter how careful she was; a large chunk was now missing from the back of the baby's head. The young woman threw the gum wrapped in the curly brown hair into the trash can.

"I'm just glad it wasn't a piece of candy or something dangerous." She put the scissors on the dresser. That was the first swing, and then came the second. "Maybe when I'm not here we should leave her with my mother."

Wallace was waiting for that. He was surprised only that it had taken this long before she said it. In recent months she had been much quicker with her insults and innuendoes. He looked at his wife, trying to think of the right thing to say. She sighed, rolling her eyes, and took Hope from him. Without an answer to satisfy her, he shrugged his shoulders helplessly and left the room.

Lana knew she should go after him, knew it wasn't a big deal, knew that gum stuck in a baby's hair wasn't worth this amount of anger and tension, knew that this was an opportunity to create some goodwill between them. But after the disastrous mountain trip and after so many months of false apologies, she, just like Wallace, had run out of ways to say she was sorry.

He was in the kitchen, the cabinets opening and slamming, and she shut the door. She put the baby in the crib and sat down on the floor, her back against the wall. She thought about her life, trying to measure how far things had gotten, trying to count the steps she would need to take to get to the place she once had been.

She faced the open window, the crisp winter night sky full of stars and the distant sounds of traffic, and tried to imagine that she was happy, that she was settled and at peace. Pretending that she was living the life she had always wanted to live, she tried to find a thread of pleasure inside her; but she could find nothing of hope or delight. All that was there was unrecognizable, unimagined, and the pieces were tangled and gnarled, her heart a tight web of disappointment.

Early in the marriage Lana had convinced herself that any difficulty she and Wallace would face would come from the outside, from prejudiced people who didn't understand their love, from those who would try to pull them apart, claiming that they were too young, too different, too immature. Displeasure and regret and the tickle of wondering what might have been were intimate foes for which neither Lana nor Wallace had readied themselves, and now they wrestled to survive.

Lana leaned back and closed her eyes, remembering the recent trip. A desperate attempt to shore up the marriage, the trip to the mountains was intended to be a weekend of romance and rest and reconciliation. They could be alone, without the baby, without family, and reclaim the love they once believed could weather any storm. Instead, it had turned into three days of increasing clarity that the gap between them was deep and steady and formidable.

They left Hope with her parents and took off early Friday morning. With a full tank of gas and a stack of old cassette tapes, they drove out of town listening to the music they had discovered together and enjoyed in the early days of their dating. Wallace turned up the heat, and they rolled all the windows down, the cool breeze dancing across them, the sun high and bright. Lana seemed easy with him, singing the songs, reclining in the seat, and once even reaching across, touching him gently on the leg.

They talked of old friends, a wedding that was planned in

the spring and how Wallace was pleased with his job as a night clerk. They discussed Jessie and James going to Africa and where they might go if they planned a trip of a lifetime. She said Australia and he agreed, and they considered the things they would do, the various places they would visit. They laughed about how his grandparents seemed so young and in love the days before their departure, and he mentioned how he hoped that they might feel the same at their age.

She smiled when he told her how good she looked in that same old pair of jeans she had worn the winter before she was pregnant, how she still had the sexiest figure. After about two hours on the road, she even closed her eyes, falling asleep on his shoulder; and Wallace began to think that a trip had been all the relationship needed, that it was the cure, the remedy. He thought that just having a chance to be alone without their daughter or parents or grandparents was going to bridge the gap that had opened between them. He congratulated himself that they had only needed the opportunity to drive out and away from those things that had become too familiar, a chance to forget what had only recently come to pass.

But once they arrived at the hotel, once the door was shut and they were alone together, once he put his arms around her and tried to show how much he cared for her, she grew stiff and distant, claiming she was tired and wanted to sleep.

In the past he would not have pushed her; he always retreated, giving her the space she requested. But after the free and easy trip they had just enjoyed, the light conversation, the way they fell into the gentle fashion of how things used to be, he was so hopeful, so expectant, so sure they were on the right path, he couldn't give up.

"Come on, baby," he said, sliding his hands down her back, trying to undo her bra.

They kissed and he felt her loosen.

"You feel so good. I've missed you. I've missed making love to you."

She was hesitant. It had been almost six months since they had been together, and she had been relieved when finally, after so many nights of being denied, he had quit asking. She worried that if she relented this time she would have to go back to the constant struggle they endured in bed. They would have to return to what had been the most unsettling part of her melancholy, the most awkward part of her discontent.

She hated saying no to Wallace. She hated herself for not feeling what she believed should be natural for a wife to feel about a husband. She was ashamed that she considered sleeping with another man when she knew her husband would do anything she wanted, try anything she requested.

The sex between Lana and Wallace had been good for both of them since they had been together, so it wasn't that she had become dissatisfied. She simply was not interested in making love, not with her husband, not with anybody. Roger, the man she was seeing, was just a means to flee the constant ache of loneliness, a distraction from the emptiness inside her. Roger didn't necessarily please or excite her. But the game was interesting. At least with him, when she refused to get a hotel room or slip away to his apartment, she did not feel guilty or improper. At least when she denied his advances she could feel good about herself, feel some pride in her choice. At least when she said no to him she felt like she was doing the right thing, which was so unlike how she felt at home.

When she tried to figure it out for herself, Lana didn't know how she lost had her drive. She wasn't sure what had caused the break inside her. She did not understand how such a thing had happened, but she certainly knew when it had happened. During her nine months of pregnancy, the desire, the arousal, the need for intimacy gradually wrapped itself around Hope; and when the time came, it labored and slid out with her at birth, leaving Lana barren and bereft of passion. She pretended that she wanted to get close to Wallace. She acted like she needed him but after almost two years, she had faked all the longing she could.

As he stood there in front of her, his heart beating so fast she felt his racing pulse more strongly than she felt her own, she realized that he was desperately trying to save the marriage, desperately trying to hold on to what they had, desperately trying to get close. So she softened and decided to try as well.

There, away from home, surrounded by the dark mountains, a green fence holding them both in, she decided to let him inside her again, to see if maybe there was something that had not been lost or stolen or smashed, something that might bind them back together.

After all, she had enjoyed the lightness of the trip too, the ease with which she had napped. She had liked being alone with him in the car, no baby in the backseat, the two of them free and driving out of town. She had enjoyed the conversation, the interested way he spoke to her, the confidence he exhibited behind the wheel. So she chose to let him hold her, let him be close to her. She gently pushed him away and began taking off her clothes. Wallace moved the suitcase off the bed, lay down, and watched as she undressed. He was overcome with desire and pulled her into himself and, with great affection, began making love.

Lana willed herself to be ready. She lay aside the sorrow, ignored the pang of disillusion. She calmly and faithfully resisted the urge to jump up and run away. The young wife, in a grand attempt to please her husband and fortify their marriage, steadied herself, preparing her soul, her mind, her body for the reunion. She tried to open herself, make room for him, create a space in the twisted knot that was her heart; but she quickly recognized her failure.

The weight of his body on top of her, the frenzy of his excitement, the desperate push and pull of him inside her, launched Lana even deeper into the disappointment she could not name. By the time he was finished, exploding in unrestrained pleasure, Lana had retreated further into herself, and the space between them had widened.

Wallace opened his eyes and looked down at her as she lay beneath him. Clearly unaware of how far they had drifted away from each other, clearly unsuspecting of how tangled and jumbled his wife's thoughts and feelings had become, he expected to find the girl he had first loved.

He expected to find the familiar sweetness of delight and the way she used to shine. He expected it all to be suddenly and completely all right, but in that one glance he now understood that neither the drive and the music nor the holding of hands, the nap on the shoulder, the ease of the summer day, the time alone, even the intimacy of sex—none of it would be enough to reclaim all that had been lost. Whatever had pulled them apart from each other had polarized them, frozen them in positions with no visible way back to each other.

He got up and walked into the bathroom, shutting the door behind him. He showered while Lana rolled over, the sheets cold and stiff.

They spent the rest of the weekend speaking only of topics chosen with care, superficial subjects, polite conversation. They did not touch each other again, sleeping restlessly at the edges of the bed, and they drove home painfully aware the neither of them had a clue as to what might save them.

"I'll be late," he yelled from beyond the room. And the front door slammed shut.

Lana waited a few minutes before getting up, the quiet and emptiness in the house settling around her. She went over and shut the window and returned to the crib while Hope lay down without any direction or assistance from her mother. The baby's smile dulled once she realized that her father had left, and the young woman started to tell herself that her daughter's lack of affection toward her was one more sign that Wallace had poisoned everything in her life.

She wanted to say that it was Wallace's fault that she felt so unloving toward and unloved by their daughter. In the beginning she tried to make herself believe that he was the cause of her misery, both as a mother and as a woman. She wanted nothing more than to say that he was to blame for the fact that she wanted to leave everything, him, the marriage, their baby, the town, that he was the reason she could no longer cry. But even when she first began to feel so broken, she knew she was being unfair. She understood that the indictment she placed on her husband was undeserved and improper.

None of her trouble was his fault. It wasn't anyone's fault. She simply could no longer find the path that at one time had been so clear. She did not know how or why, but she suddenly found herself in unfamiliar and perilous territory, and when she tried to remember what she was doing, where she was going, how she got to where she was, she realized she had lost her way.

"Go to sleep," she instructed Hope and left the room. She reached up and turned off the light and walked down the hall toward the kitchen.

She was collecting and stacking the dirty dishes when she looked on the table and noticed an envelope stuck behind the napkin holder. She pulled it out and saw that it was a letter from Mrs. Jenkins to Wallace, something his grandmother must have written before she left. Lana put the dishes down and opened it as if it were also addressed to her.

Dear Wallace,

I know I've left you all the instructions about taking care of the house; and I know that everything will be fine while your grandfather and I will be gone. I just wanted to say a few things to you before I leave.

I got a bad feeling, Wallace, and I can't seem to shake it. I've tried to get clear-headed enough to know who it concerns, but I don't have anything but the feeling. No understanding to go with it. Maybe it's like what folks say, just traveling nerves and maybe everything will be fine. But I needed to say some things to somebody in the family in case the badness happens to me on the trip. So I decided to write it to you, the oldest grandson, the father of my great-grandbaby, and the one living in my house.

First of all, I want you to know that I'm real proud of you. I don't know how you manage everything, but somehow you do. And it just goes to show what a fine man you've become. Second, I'm glad you married Lana. She's a good girl and she loves you, and, well, there's no need to even say anything about little Hope. That baby has been the light of my life this past couple of years, and she's the real reason I'm writing this letter.

What I most need to say is that I've lived a good life and I'm happy. And I just want to make sure that my children and my grandchildren and my great-grandchildren under-stand that even though all my years haven't been easy and I know I've made plenty of mistakes, I feel at peace for the way things have gone.

I love your grandfather and it's a blessing to me that he's come home. I cannot pretend I understand why he left and why we spent so much of life apart, but I've learned over the years that a person doesn't get to choose their sorrow. Like the weather, it just comes.

I'm writing this letter because I want my great-grandbaby to know that nothing about life is easy. That more often than not, the sunshine doesn't last and the nights can go on forever. People you trust disappoint you, and love is not al-ways enough. But in spite of what you lose or gain or take or give, it's all worth it. It's the living itself that's the gift.

I turned sixty last birthday, and for the first time I see more years behind me than I do in front of me; and though it saddens me to think it's almost over, I am grateful for every day I've had. Good, bad, unbearable, every day was a blessing.

I travel now to Africa, and I hope my bad feeling is nothing more than a case of separation anxiety. Because even though there's more yesterdays than there are tomor-rows, it doesn't mean I'm done.

Take care, Wallace, take care to love fiercely and to live completely. It all goes by faster than you'd think.

> With all my love,
> your grandmother, Jessie

Lana folded the letter and stuck it in the envelope. She replaced it where she had found it, standing between the napkin holder and the salt and pepper shakers, and then finished stacking dishes. She thought about Jessie and her kindness toward her, how she had welcomed them into her home, without hesitation or criticism. Mrs. Jenkins had been good to Lana, and the young woman knew it; and now, having read such an intimate and loving letter, Lana felt a deep regret that she was hurting more than just her own family.

She opened the cabinet, got out the dishwashing detergent, turned on the water, and began filling the sink. She placed the dirty flatware, the knives and cooking spoons, the measuring cup, and Hope's plastic fork into the water and wondered how long it would be before she would leave.

It wasn't that she loved Roger, the teacher in her accounting class at school whom she had met before she dropped out. He was older and had money, drove a nice car, and could speak two languages. He wore silk shirts made in Italy and insisted that she get dessert when they went out to eat. He was interesting and had traveled to China, read women's magazines, and thought she could be a model.

But Lana understood that she wasn't leaving Wallace for him. She wasn't abandoning her marriage and her baby because she had fallen in love with somebody else. He wasn't the reason for all that she was feeling. She only wished it could be that simple. That was understandable, even acceptable. Friends and family would be able to explain that to each other. It could be the hook for everything else to hang on.

She'd be hated and despised for what she had done, but at least they'd think they had a handle on why she left. There would be a reason, an explanation. They would all shake their heads with disgust but not confusion. Lana wished all that she was feeling could be summed up so cleanly. But it wasn't that easy. It wasn't that simple.

Lana realized that, just as Wallace was not to be blamed for her unhappiness, this other man was not everything she was missing. He, like her husband, was not the reason she was running away. Although she enjoyed the attention he gave her, found relief in the distraction of the new relationship, and appreciated having to put forth an effort to keep things secret, the young woman knew it was not enough to fix all that was wrong. She understood that Roger was just a balm, a Band-Aid, an excuse. Lana even knew that she would not stay with him for very long before she would go again. He was merely the convenient means to help her leave.

The young woman was finishing washing the pots and pans when she heard the doorbell ring and looked over at the kitchen clock to see that it was after 9:00 P.M. She dried her hands on the dish towel, walked over to the entryway, pulled aside the curtain on the window beside the door, and saw Margaret Peele standing on the porch. She unlocked and opened the door, and the older woman was smiling in front of her, holding a box of cocoa.

"It's not too late, is it?" the woman asked.

Lana shook her head in surprise. "Um, I was cleaning up a

bit," she answered and then realized she should ask her former Sunday school teacher to come in.

She stood back, pulling the door with her. Margaret walked in.

"I was just thinking of you and decided to stop by." She spoke a little nervously. "I remember how much you used to like hot chocolate." She lifted up the box in her hand. "Sorry, but it's instant."

"Oh, that's all right," Lana responded. "That's really nice of you." The young woman shut the door. "Here, let me take that." And she reached behind Margaret and pulled off her coat. "Wallace just left and Hope's gone to bed." She opened the closet and took out a hanger, hung up Margaret's coat, and shut the door.

"Then it's just you and me," the visitor said as she turned around to face Lana.

"Yeah, I guess so," the young woman replied. "Come on in the kitchen while I heat up the water." And she moved ahead of Margaret toward the other room.

"I haven't seen you in a couple of weeks. Did you and Wallace go away?" The older woman followed her into the kitchen.

Lana dried one of the pots she had just washed and turned on the water. She filled two cups and then emptied them in the pot and placed it on the stove. She turned the dial to high.

"Let's see," she said to answer the question, "two weeks ago Hope was sick with a virus so we didn't go to church that

Sunday, and then last week Wallace and I went to the mountains."

"Oh, that sounds like a nice trip," Margaret responded. "Did you ski?"

Lana shook her head, remembering the brief discussion they'd had about the cost of skiing. Wallace had wanted to try it, but Lana had said it was too expensive.

Margaret sat down at the table and Lana joined her. Neither woman appeared to know what to say. There was an awkward pause.

Finally Margaret asked, "Have you heard from Jessie?"

Lana nodded, glad to have an easy topic of conversation.

"She called when they got to London and then also after they checked into their hotel in Nairobi." Lana hoped she said the town in Kenya correctly. She wasn't sure how to pronounce it. Then she finished, "They're both fine. Tired, but fine."

"That's a long trip."

"Twenty-two hours, she said." Lana shook her head. "I think I'd go crazy on a plane that long."

Margaret agreed with a nod.

Lana got up from the table and opened the packets of hot chocolate. She emptied the contents into two mugs and then waited until the water started to boil. She took the pot off the stove and poured the water into the cups. Then she put the pot in the sink and got out a spoon and stirred both drinks. She handed her visitor a cup, and the women blew across the top, trying to cool down the liquid.

"Reminds me of old times," Margaret said before she took a sip.

Lana smiled, trying to recall an occasion when she had drunk hot chocolate with the older woman.

Margaret could tell Lana was puzzled, so she said, "When you first found out you were pregnant, remember?"

Lana put down her cup.

"You came over to the house and we talked and then we went over to your mom's."

Lana didn't respond.

"We had hot chocolate."

The younger woman started to think back to that night she had gone to see Mrs. Peele. She certainly had memories of going to her house, how it felt finally to have made the decision to tell an adult, how frightened she was to let somebody know what had happened. The evening seemed so long ago to her now, and though she did remember the occasion of her confession, she did not recall drinking hot chocolate.

"I used to make it from scratch," Margaret said, hoping that might spark a memory.

Nothing. Lana just sat watching.

"Well, it doesn't matter," the older woman finally said. "Two friends don't have to remember doing something earlier to enjoy it at a later time." And she took another sip.

Lana smiled and nodded.

There was another awkward hesitation between them.

"How's your health, Mrs. Peele?" Lana inquired, unsure of whether she should ask but uncomfortable with the silence.

"I went to the doctor a couple of days ago. I'm cancer free!" she said and lifted her cup as if she had given a toast.

"That's great," Lana responded.

"Better than great," Margaret answered.

"Yes, you must be so relieved." And the young woman pulled out a couple of napkins and pushed one toward Margaret.

The two women sat in silence, both of them trying to think of something to say, one of them tangled in what she had seen and the other one caught in what she had done. They sipped their chocolate and listened to the sounds of the furnace coming on and the passing of an airplane overhead.

Margaret struggled with how to begin. She had thought about what she would say all the previous day and night and all that morning. She had practiced how she might broach the subject with the young woman, how she might ask if things were okay. She worried that she might be out of line. She had rehearsed an opening and an easy way to allow Lana to talk if she wanted to. But now that she was there with her, now that they were alone, drinking cocoa and talking of gentler subjects, Margaret was at a loss as to how to say what she hoped was the right thing.

She put down her mug, slid her chair away from the table, and simply began. She jumped in headfirst and long.

"Lana, have I ever told you about Luther?" Margaret folded her hands in her lap.

"Your husband?" Lana asked.

Margaret nodded. "He died before you were born."

Lana shook her head. "No, I can't say as I ever remember you talking about him."

"We were married almost thirty years," Margaret said. "Hard to believe it was that long." And she reached up and rubbed the back of her neck. "He was a farmer, raised chickens. He was a good man."

The young woman took another sip from her mug of chocolate. She tried not to appear guilty.

The older woman smiled, dropping her hand in her lap, and turned to Lana. "We got married fairly young," she said, taking a breath. And then she told it straight. "I left him after we had been together three and a half years." She waited. "It wasn't that he was a bad man or that things changed. He didn't do anything to hurt me. And, well, I really didn't stay gone for very long."

She paused, still watching Lana, the young woman staring into her cup.

"I guess I just worried that I had made a mistake, that our relationship wasn't quite everything that I thought marriage was supposed to be. I felt, I don't know," then she turned away from the younger woman, remembering, "smothered or lost or something."

Lana closed her eyes, the light in the kitchen suddenly starting to bother her.

"I left him on a Thursday," she said. "In June." She glanced beside them, out the window. "It was so hot I could hardly breathe. I packed my bags and took a bus to Memphis." The older woman stopped a minute, thinking about her past as she dealt her memories out like cards on the table.

"I even went to a bar and had a drink with a stranger." She leaned forward and picked her cup off the table and took a sip. "It was all so very exciting." She turned back toward her friend, whose face was still cast downward.

"Anyway, by Sunday I realized that Memphis didn't have what I was really looking for, so I got on a bus and came home." Margaret ran her finger along the top of her cup. "I never left again."

She wiped her hand on the napkin. She wasn't even sure Lana was listening.

Finally, the young woman responded. Her voice sounded small, distant. "What did your husband do?"

"Met me at the bus station, had a little bouquet of daisies." She stopped as if to recall. "Told me that he hadn't slept in three nights and that he was sorry if he had done something wrong."

Margaret sat leaning in her chair with her cup in her hands, remembering how her husband had stood waiting for her at the bus terminal. She thought of how it was to see him through the window on the bus as they pulled up, how he was out front all alone, his hat resting on his forehead, perspiration running down the sides of his face, the heaviness in his eyes and all along his shoulders.

"In all of the rest of the years that we were married, there was nothing that he did that made me love him more than I loved him that day." She brought the chocolate to her mouth and drank the last swallow. "He never asked me why I left or what I did while I was away or if I thought I'd leave again." She sat forward and put her cup on the table. Then she slid her chair back and rested her chin on the palms of her hands. "He just welcomed me home. He handed me those five little stems of yellow flowers, reached out, took my luggage, and welcomed me back home."

Margaret remembered the day she returned, how hot the vinyl on the seat in Luther's truck was and how he pulled her away from the door before she got in, took a towel from behind the seat, folded it, and draped it across where she would sit.

She remembered how the sweat beaded across the top of her lip, how a strand of her hair kept sticking across her eyes, and how he turned to her at the end of the road just before their driveway. She thought he would ask if she really meant to be home.

She remembered the smell of grass, the white clouds, and the taste of salt on his neck when she leaned over to kiss him. She remembered the strength of his hand on her leg and the pink and lavender snapdragons blooming at the front porch of their house, the reflection of the sun on the tin roof and the way Luther opened his door and reached for her across the seat. She remembered being happy and sad at the same time, how it felt to leave and then come back. Empty in some places, filled up in others.

Margaret turned her attention to her friend.

"See, the thing about being restless is that it isn't about who you're married to or where you run off to." She wasn't sure she was saying the right thing, but she kept going. "It isn't about anybody else and what you feel for them or don't feel for them." She interlaced her fingers, her hands readied for prayer.

"What I'm trying to say is that a person never finds what's missing from their lives in somebody else. Or in Memphis," Margaret added, thinking of her own displeasure and departure from home.

"I felt stuck in those early years, edgy and unfulfilled, but I didn't feel those things because of the man I married or because of where I lived." She swallowed and then finished. "I felt that way because I had not come to terms with what was inside my heart."

Lana did not speak.

Margaret continued. "So, when I came home I did that. I listened to my heart. I tried finding out how I felt about things, and it was hard at first because nobody ever taught me how. I never knew a person could feel things so deeply like sorrow or anger or disappointment and then cover them up with indifference or frustration. I thought you grow up, you do the things you've been told to do, you go to work, you eat and sleep and make a life for yourself, and that the happiness, the fulfillment that everybody else seems to have, would just show up. I never knew you had to choose to be happy, choose to find out who you are in the midst of all those days of doing what you think you're supposed to do. I never realized that peace is what you find when you're able to sit with all the parts that are your life, all the fears and surprises and mistakes and regrets and all those fine, perfect moments of being loved and say to yourself, 'This is a glorious life.'"

Margaret shifted in her seat, hooking her feet around the legs of the chair. She knew the young woman felt accused, convicted, and she struggled with how to go on since the truth seemed like such a slippery notion.

"Now, Lana, I'll be the first one to admit that I'm no marriage expert, and I know that there are situations where it's better to split up than stay together." And here she stopped, trying to be careful. "But I don't believe a person can know that without spending some time sitting with herself, alone. A person can't figure those big things out if her head is full of distractions, even tall, dark, good-looking ones."

Lana fidgeted in discomfort, and Margaret worried that she had spoken too much and that she had only made things worse. She waited, trying to think of something else to say, but there was nothing.

She stood up, preparing to leave, noticing the familiar cloak of discontent that hung about the young woman, the air of misery and the uncertain glaze behind the eyes.

She hesitated a minute and then spoke. "Well, I'm sorry to have gone on so long with my silly story. I know you're needing your sleep." Standing behind her chair, she placed her hands on the top of it. "But, Lana, I just want you to know," and she said this very seriously, "if you ever need me for anything, to talk, to baby-sit, to ride with you to Memphis, you know you can call me, anytime." And she pushed her chair under the table and walked from the room to get her coat out of the closet.

Lana waited and then got up from her chair just as Margaret was opening the front door. She held it as the older woman walked out onto the porch.

"Anytime," Margaret repeated to the young mother, who watched from inside the house, still silenced by what was shared.

Margaret turned and walked down the steps and headed to her car. She stood beside her door and waved good-bye. Lana remained inside, holding up one hand as a greeting, and with the other she reached across her chest, covering the gaping hole that was her heart.

Six

THE PILOT NEWS

Dear Aunt Dot,

I work in a place where there is a lot of cigarette smoke. I find that it's in my hair and my clothes. Any ideas on how to take out that smoky smell?

Butt-Tired

Dear Butt,

Maybe you ought to think about finding another place to work because the stains and residue you find on the outside are probably on the inside too. Read up on the dangers of secondhand smoke. OK, enough of a lecture: white vinegar is your answer. Put it in with your laundry and even your shampoo. It will take away the smell of tobacco smoke.

"You smoke?" Lamont opened the glove compartment and found the pack of cigarettes.

"No," Charlotte replied, turning to see what the teenager was doing in her things.

"You used to smoke?" He pulled it out, noticing that the pack had been opened.

"No, never did," she answered as she switched on the turn signal and changed lanes.

"You got a boyfriend who smokes?" He took a cigarette out and stuck it in his mouth and plugged in the lighter.

"No, and I really wish you wouldn't do that in my car." She yanked out the lighter.

Lamont took the cigarette out of his mouth and stuck it in the front pocket of his shirt. He turned to the driver as if he was waiting for an explanation.

Charlotte could tell that he was watching her. She looked over and then back to face the road. She felt a bit apprehensive having the young man in her car. She wasn't frightened of him or worried that he might hurt her; she just felt a little nervous having him so close.

Peggy had come by the parsonage with the bail money and asked that Charlotte get him out. The grandmother claimed that she couldn't go because she didn't have anyone to stay with her husband and that she needed the extra time to clean out the bedroom where Lamont would be sleeping.

There had been a fight with Sherry about letting the teenager move in with his grandparents. His mother had said to let him stay in jail, that maybe that would teach him a lesson. But Peggy had listened to too many late-night phone calls from her grandson when he begged to be released and promised to stay away from trouble. She had talked it over with her husband and they agreed that he could stay with them.

"He can help me out with Vastine," Peggy explained as she handed the cashier's check to Charlotte. "I could use some extra support." And she thanked the reluctant pastor and hurried out the door before she could be denied.

Charlotte called the jail chaplain and the magistrate to find out what she needed to do, then she reluctantly drove to Winston-Salem, filled out the paperwork; and it wasn't long before the young man was out of jail and sitting in her car. It was almost an hour's drive back to Hope Springs.

"They're for the Cigarette Lady," Charlotte said, to answer his questions. "And you shouldn't be going through my glove compartment without me saying it's all right." She pushed her foot on the gas pedal and got the speed where she wanted it and hit the cruise button.

"You're right," he said apologetically. "I'm sorry." He crossed his legs at his ankles. Then after thinking a minute he asked, "Who's the Cigarette Lady?"

Charlotte thought about the elderly lady who lived out on the edge of the community near the church. She had first encountered her three or four years earlier.

"She's this old woman who stands at the end of her driveway, flagging down cars trying to find somebody who smokes." She reached up and pulled at her shoulder strap.

"Apparently, she runs out of cigarettes quite a bit, and since she doesn't drive and the store is too far away for her to walk, she bums the only way she knows how."

"In the middle of the road?" Lamont asked with a note of surprise.

"Yep, in the middle of the road," Charlotte responded.

"Damn," the young man said, and then he covered his mouth with his hand when he remembered he was with a preacher. "Sorry," he added.

"It's okay," she said with assurance. Then she looked at him again. She noticed that he seemed jumpy too. She plugged the lighter back in.

"Go ahead and smoke," she told him.

He angled himself so that he could face the minister. Once again, she felt him watching her.

"What?" she asked.

"I was just wondering why you give the old woman cancer sticks."

The lighter popped and he pulled it out and lit the cigarette he had taken from his front shirt pocket and stuck it between his lips. He sucked in a deep breath and returned it. Then he finished what he was saying.

"I mean, I thought preachers don't like smoking." He let his window down a bit.

Charlotte glanced up to see the cars in the rearview mirror and then caught a glimpse of the boy sitting next to her. He was drawing in the smoke hard and deeply. She stared straight ahead as she drove.

"It does harm the body," she said, "and I suppose it's not a good thing because of that." Charlotte began to chew on the inside of her lip as she thought about the old woman and giving her cigarettes. She stopped talking and remembered the last time she had driven down the road where the old woman lived and seen her.

It was just after Christmas and the elderly lady was standing very close to the road, wearing a thin bathrobe and men's slippers. She had an old wool scarf thrown around her neck, and her hair was uncombed, her mouth still a little dirty from an earlier meal. Charlotte had pulled over and rolled down the passenger's side window, and the woman had stuck the whole upper part of her body inside and leaned across the seat.

"Hey, sweetie," she had said, her voice loud and raspy, the words spoken slowly and deliberately, as if she had to think through every syllable. "You don't smoke, do you?" she asked as she sniffed inside the car, not remembering the previous times Charlotte had stopped.

"No, ma'am," the minister had answered, "but I bought you a pack of Marlboros." And she reached into the glove compartment and handed the old woman the pack.

"No, I just need a couple," she'd always say. "Cleo promised to take me to the store this evening. I'll buy my own then." And she took out three, maybe four, cigarettes and handed the pack back to the driver.

"I sure do appreciate it, though," she said as she pulled herself away from the car. "You take care now, honey," she added as she waved good-bye.

And then Charlotte watched as the old woman walked to her house, waved a final time, went inside, and shut the door.

It was always the easiest bit of ministry the young pastor performed.

Several times she thought maybe she should stop by and make a visit, check on the lady when she wasn't standing by the side of the road, find out if Cleo was really somebody who took care of her. She had even considered asking the church women if they knew who she was and if she needed assistance from the community.

But then she decided that she liked the anonymity in their relationship. That she liked only knowing her as the Cigarette Lady and she herself being seen not as a pastor but only as some passerby with Marlboros in her car. It satisfied the minister to be able just to give her what she asked for, just to take care of that one need, sinful or not, just to benefit the desire of one old woman and then let it be.

It was simple and tidy. An old woman needed a cigarette. Charlotte gave her one. She liked how it felt not to have to worry if the thing she had given was the right thing. There was a wish and she had made it come true. It wasn't at all like she felt after she prayed, when she wondered whether the prayer she had offered was done so in the right way, whether or not she had brought comfort to a broken heart or appeased a God she could never fully understand. She didn't have to agonize about the exchange of this gift like she did after every sermon, unsure if she had even gotten close to revealing a message of hope.

There was no second-guessing or sense of failure like she often felt. So many times it seemed she had been called upon to bring a great and miraculous staff like Moses used to separate the waters and create a way out of no way, and instead she had shown up with only a snorkel, evidence of her disbelief. She found contentment in this situation unlike she could find anywhere else because she knew what somebody wanted and she was able to give it to her. So, sin or no sin, giving the old woman a cigarette was one of the few times during the week when Charlotte felt as if she had done a good thing.

The pastor returned her attention to the teenager's earlier question. "Some preachers do preach against smoking, claim it's the devil's business. Others would say it's harmful to the temple of God, while some might say it's an indulgence of the flesh." She paused, remembering all the sermons she had heard that included speaking about cigarettes.

"But there's others who don't preach about it because they know too many in their congregation enjoy a smoke once in a while or because they realize that most of the money that comes in the plate on Sunday morning is there because of tobacco farming; so I would say that not all preachers would call smoking a sin."

"That why you give the old woman cigarettes, because it supports tobacco farming?" He drew in a long breath.

"No," she responded. "I give them to her because that's all she asks for."

The young man nodded as if he understood, as if what the pastor was saying made complete sense.

They rode for a while in silence as Lamont pondered his new life, going back to a place he had almost forgotten. He wasn't sure how long he would be able to stay away from a city or from a place where he could buy what he needed to take the edge off how he was feeling.

He had promised his grandmother that he would live with them, help take care of his grandfather, stay with him so that she could get out once in a while, that he would even drive them around town, to appointments and church. And when he had made the promise, he had thought it was completely possible to maintain such an existence, but now that he was heading in that direction, the nicotine not enough to stop his fidgeting, he understood that he would probably soon be breaking another promise.

It wasn't like he enjoyed himself when he did it. It wasn't like his mother said, that he was mean and didn't care. He really wanted to do right, he really desired to keep the vows he had made. It just was too hard. Living without the high was just too hard.

"There's NA meetings at the Lutheran church in Hope Springs," Charlotte said as if she was reading his mind.

"You got junkies in Hope Springs?" He crushed the cigarette butt in the ashtray and rubbed his hands together.

"I wouldn't know. I don't go to the meetings," she answered. "But I do know they've been going on for several years, so somebody must be attending."

"Maybe it's the preacher," the teenager said lightly. "Maybe he gives out pot to the Joint Lady."

Charlotte laughed. "Yeah, that's probably what it is. A twelve-step cover-up for a minister's dealing."

"Never know," he responded. "One gives out cigarettes, another gives weed."

"No, it's true; you never know," Charlotte answered.

Lamont opened the glove compartment and pulled out another cigarette. "You'll have to tell the old woman that I smoked all her sticks." He pushed in the lighter, waited, and then lit his cigarette.

"So, what's the matter with Granddaddy?" he asked Charlotte.

She noticed the clock on the dashboard. It was almost four in the afternoon. She hoped they were early enough to miss the commute traffic.

"Congestive heart failure," she replied. "He's been sick a long time."

Lamont had not seen his grandfather in almost five years. He had rarely come back to Hope Springs since moving in with his mother. He hadn't visited in spite of the numerous requests he had received.

"Is he going to die?" He tapped the cigarette in the ashtray.

"He's a hospice patient," she replied. "Do you know what that means?"

The young man shook his head and took another drag.

"It's an agency that works with terminally ill people. They gave him a prognosis." She stopped and decided to use simpler words. "They say he only has about six months to live." She stared straight ahead.

Lamont nodded with his whole body and twisted his neck to watch the fields and businesses as they sped past.

He was quiet then, didn't ask any more about his grandfather or how he was. He sat and counted the cars passing, saw the restaurants and strip malls, how much things had changed since he'd lived in that area.

"Did they tell you when your court date is?" Charlotte asked.

He shook his head. "I guess it's written on those papers they gave me, but I didn't read them." He put out the cigarette and slouched down in his seat.

They drove on further, getting closer to Hope Springs.

"Why did Granny send you to get me?" he asked, the question bothering him for most of the drive.

Charlotte shrugged her shoulders. She hadn't really considered the reasoning for Peggy's request. "She said she couldn't get anyone to stay with Vastine and that she needed to clean out your bedroom."

Lamont nodded. "You think she's afraid of me?"

Charlotte watched as a car came up very close behind them and then pulled around. She checked her speedometer and guessed that it had to have been going almost a hundred miles per hour. She couldn't believe drivers drove with such carelessness.

"I don't know, Lamont," she answered. "I don't think she liked going to visit you at the jail very much." She brought one hand down and rested it on the gearshift between the two seats. "But I suppose that if she was really afraid of you, she wouldn't be letting you stay at her house."

Lamont thought about that. He wanted another cigarette but felt embarrassed to take a third one out of the pack.

"I never had no gun," he said to the preacher as if she had asked. "Somebody else stuck that under my seat when the cops stopped us." He pulled his hands along the sides of his head. "I ain't never agreed to using no guns."

Charlotte didn't know what to say to the teenager; she wasn't sure what he wanted from her, where he was going with this line of conversation. So she was silent.

"We had decided to pull something simple. Nobody was supposed to be there and nobody was going to get hurt. We just needed some money for a party." He stuck his fingers through the open window as if he was testing to see how cold it was or to feel the wind on his skin.

"I said I'd never be with nobody who used guns." He pulled his hand in. He wondered how long he could wait before taking another cigarette.

"Why would you think your grandmother is afraid of you?" Charlotte finally asked.

Lamont explained sharply, "Well, that doesn't take a genius to figure out, does it? A grandson in jail who steals, who's been caught with a gun? The church ladies must love that." He gripped the handle on the car door.

"I don't think the church ladies know," Charlotte said, noticing how nervous he seemed.

"Yeah, right. Like everybody in that small town doesn't know everybody else's secrets," he replied.

Charlotte thought about it. She wasn't sure what anybody else knew about Peggy and Vastine's situation. No one had mentioned anything to her, but that didn't always mean they were without information. Sometimes they were a little careful with their gossip around the preacher.

"So?" Charlotte said. "Even if the church ladies do know, what difference does that make?" She changed hands, resting one in her lap. "If your grandmother didn't want you to come and stay with her, if she was worried about what others think, or if she really was afraid of you, she wouldn't have bailed you out, and she certainly wouldn't let you stay with them."

Finally Lamont couldn't stand it anymore. He opened the compartment at his knees, took out another cigarette. Charlotte watched as he lit it, taking another long, drawn-out breath as he sucked in the smoke.

"You ever done anything you're ashamed of?" He pulled the cigarette out of his mouth and studied the way it was made. He rolled it around in his fingers, noticing the straight tight line where the paper was glued, the compact way the ashes stayed together as the fire burned along the edges.

Charlotte thought about the question. She cracked her window to let out some of the smoke that had collected in the car. Lamont opened the window more on his side, following suit.

The minister realized that she had known lots of emotions—disappointment, sorrow, regret, fear, anger. Many of these feelings she had discussed with Marion. They had spent months of sessions dealing with her issues about her sister's death, her mother's alcoholism, and her father's abandonment. They had talked of her ministry and the depressed way she felt when she attempted the work of a pastor.

They analyzed her dreams, the sense of loss and dread that stayed with her, and the slight pressure of sadness that always lay upon her heart. They spoke of unfulfilled dreams, clinging to the past, and how much pain one person can bear. But in all their conversations, in all their moments of clarity and insight, in all of Marion's wise renderings and Charlotte's vulnerable sharing, they had never spoken of shame.

Of course, Charlotte thought, I have felt ashamed of my mother's drinking and my father's disappearance. Of course, she thought, I have been ashamed of how Serena died and how I wasn't there with her when it happened. I have been ashamed of the things I have said at times, the moments I lashed out in anger. But as she glanced over at the young man who had asked the question, a teenager who had already fallen into the downward spiral of addiction, a young boy who had already caused his family so much pain that his mother had kicked him out of her life, she realized that she had never lost herself to that brand of sorrow.

In her careful and sober way of picking through a life, she had encountered many demons, but that was one she had never wrestled with and lost.

"No," she answered. "Not like what you're talking about."

Lamont put the cigarette to his lips and closed his eyes. He seemed appreciative of her honesty. He waited a minute, blew out a breath of smoke, and then responded. "I sold my mother's wedding band." He stuck the cigarette through the crack in the window.

Charlotte watched the road.

"I figured she wouldn't miss it anyway. She and my dad had been divorced a long time. So, I went through her jewelry and found it in a small black box in the far corner of her drawer." He rested his head against the back of his seat.

"It was a set, you know," he said, explaining. "A little diamond on one ring and another plain one that fit beneath it. There were little chips of stones all around the big one." He pulled his hand in and took another drag off the cigarette.

"I sold it to a pawn shop down near where she works. Seventy-five bucks," he said, the memory clear in his mind. "When I got home, after blowing the money, she was sitting in the middle of her bedroom, down at the foot of her bed, the drawer pulled out, all the jewelry scattered on the floor, the little black box on her lap, open and empty." The teenager thumped the cigarette out the window. "She had been crying but she wasn't then. She just looked up at me while I was standing at the door. Just looked up at me."

Charlotte took the exit off the interstate, heading into Hope Springs.

"Then she said to me all soft and lonely sounding, 'Don't matter anyway; he ain't coming back.'" Lamont spoke quietly, his voice stretched and thin. "That was the worst time," he added, his confession finished.

Charlotte drove without responding. She wasn't sure why he had told her or if he needed something from her. It felt complete and whole in just the way it had been said.

He opened up the glove compartment to get another cigarette, and Charlotte reached over and pulled out the pack.

"Here," she said. "Just take the whole thing. I'll buy some more for the old woman."

Lamont nodded, wiped his nose with the back of his hand, and stuck the pack of cigarettes in the pocket of his coat.

She drove the rest of the way without either of them speaking. For the next seven miles they rode in silence, the air heavy with smoke. When they pulled into the driveway of his grandparents' home, they both saw Peggy watching from the front window.

They got out of the car without looking at each other.

"Thanks for the smokes," was all that the young man said. Together they walked to the door.

Seven

∗ A U N T ∗ D O T'S ∗ H E L P F U L ∗ H I N T S ∗

Dear Aunt Dot,

Is there any way to save old athletic shoes? I think mine are still sturdy. They just need a little cleaning. Can I keep them white and tidy without having to throw them in the washer?

Cheap Street-Walker

Dear Walker,

You can clean your athletic shoes in the washer or by hand. If you're more inclined to wash them by hand, just use a mixture of 1 part baking soda and 4 parts water. Use an old toothbrush to scrub hard-to-reach places. Rinse well. And make sure to stuff the shoes with towels or paper while they air-dry.

ick!" Beatrice came in from her morning walk and took off her shoes while she called out for her husband. She noticed how dirty they had gotten, and she wondered if she should go ahead and wash them right then.

"Dick?" She stood at the door and massaged the top of her right foot, which was sore and a little swollen. She had trouble with gout, but she knew that if she got out of the habit of walking, she would never pick it back up. She tried to exercise even when it hurt.

She slid out of her coat and hung it on the hook in the entryway. She dropped her keys on the counter, yelling out his name once more. "Dick?"

The house was silent and Beatrice peered through the kitchen door into the garage, noticing that her husband's car was gone. He had left while she was out on her walk. She wondered how long he had been gone, but she didn't worry because she knew that he would call before lunch and let her know where he was and if he would be joining her for the midday meal.

She blew out a breath, poured herself a glass of water, sat down at the table, and began going through the mail that he had placed there before he left.

Gerald must have come by early, she thought, noticing the clock and confirming that it was just before 10:00 A.M.

There were a couple of bills, her *Southern Living* magazine, and a newsletter from some funeral home, but she spotted the postcard right away.

It was a picture of a tiger and her cubs resting beneath a tree out on the African plains. The photograph, she guessed, appeared to have been taken late in the afternoon as the sun was low and the shadows were long and deep behind the family of cats. The cubs played at the mother's feet while the older tiger looked up, seeming to spot the photographer just as the picture was being snapped. A broad and black-striped yellow beast, she was poised but surprised that she and her family had been captured at just that moment.

Beatrice examined the picture carefully before finally turning the card over to read,

Dear Bea,
It's so amazing here. The sky is low and full, and there are moments when I feel as if I could reach out and touch a star or rest my hand upon a cloud. We've been to the village, where women sell everything they have on blankets set out on the ground. Their poverty and desperation is overwhelming. We go on the safari tomorrow. I hope this cat has already had her dinner!

Forever friends,
Jessie

Beatrice put the card in front of her nose and sniffed. It was a strange thing to do, smelling a postcard, and she wasn't sure if she was doing it because she missed Jessie and hoped to recover a familiar scent from her friend or if it was because she was curious as to whether there might be odors clinging to the picture or the words from a place she had never visited.

There were neither. It smelled like any other piece of mail that had been fingered and handled by many hands.

Disappointed, she leaned it against the fruit bowl in the middle of the table, sat back, and drank some of her water. She was hot and spent from her walk and she finished almost the entire contents of the glass before she set it down on the table.

She thought of Africa and what Jessie might be feeling being in a country so far away, the birthplace of her ancestors. Was it how it had been for her when she visited, for the first time, her great-grandparents' farm, high in the mountains of Tennessee?

She had gone with her oldest daughter, who arranged the trip for her birthday several years earlier. Beatrice had mentioned once that she had never seen the part of Tennessee where her father's people lived, and so Robin had researched the exact location of their family's whereabouts and surprised her mother with a two-day trip back home.

Once they got there, Robin decided that it was something her mother should experience alone, so she dropped Beatrice off on a street corner, giving her specific directions for finding her family's original property, and drove away, beaming with pride.

The older woman stood unmoving for a while, disoriented at first, and then walked the length of her home place end to end, now a housing development for first-time home buyers, an inexpensive but tasteful subdivision. As she walked from corner to corner, north to south, east to west, she listened to the wind and imagined that she heard the sounds of her great-grandmother calling to her children and whispering her long-ago dreams.

It had meant something to her, something deep and precious, but it had also touched a place inside her that made her feel a little lonesome. When Robin picked her up, the young woman hopeful and expectant of her mother's arranged happiness, Beatrice had not known how to talk about it. She said that she was grateful for the opportunity to go to Tennessee, back to the mountains where her bloodlines pulsed, and that it was a very thoughtful gift; but she knew that she had disappointed her daughter when she could not explain why she hadn't been completely overjoyed with the birthday present.

Was Jessie feeling some of the same emotions, joy at touching a homeland but sadness that it was no longer hers?

She sighed at her thoughts and then returned her attention to the postcard. She folded her arms across her chest, admiring the picture.

She liked the way the tiger stared right into the lens of the camera, daring and confident. It was as if she was not afraid of anything; she was bold and unswerving.

Beatrice wished that she was like that. She wished that she was strong and unmoved, unwilling to change her stance or expression when she saw a camera being pointed in her direction. She wished that she was comfortable being photographed.

She acted like she enjoyed having her picture taken, that it was a pleasure to be posed and smiling, but the truth was she hated it. She hated it because she knew that the proof of her age and sorrow would now be processed through the hands and eyes of people who did not even know her and would be examined by those she had tried to fool.

It had become disconcerting to her to be photographed ever since she had first heard about tribes of people who would not allow their pictures to be taken because they believed it captured a part of their souls. While Dick shook his head at the silliness of the superstition, Beatrice quietly believed that such a thing was possible.

She believed, in fact, that it had happened to her and that every time she had been frozen in the piece of somebody's film, beginning more than sixty years ago, when she was only a baby, a tiny edge of her spirit had been pulled away, separate and lost. By now, she thought, there must not be very much left of my soul since there are too many albums and boxes of photographs even to count.

She thought of all the occasions when her picture was taken, happy times like the births of her children, the parties and the holiday gatherings, the graduations, the anniversaries, the milestones met and passed, generation to generation. She remembered the celebrations, the ready-made smiles and steady poses she had learned and perfected over the years.

She thought about the way she felt when someone pointed the camera in her direction. And as she sat at her kitchen table, her eyes focused on the picture of a mother and her babies, a cat in Africa that was probably dead and gone now, she raised her shoulders, folded her hands in her lap, tilted her head at a slight angle, lifted the corners of her mouth, and said out loud, "Smile."

She blinked her eyes as if there had been a flash of light,

lowered herself, and leaned back in her chair. "There must be hardly any soul left," she said to a picture of a tiger and to nobody else in the room. She sat without speaking again, the image of herself frozen at the kitchen table, and remembered the event from the night before, how she had cornered her husband just after supper.

She had fixed pork chops in the large iron skillet that had been her mother's and the small English peas that Dick preferred. She tossed a salad and made sure the tea was cold and sweet before she poured it into the glasses and called him from the garage to get ready to eat.

She had cooked and prepared the table with hardly any thought of what she would discuss with him after they ate, and even though she was fixing her husband's favorite meal, it was not a part of a scheme or ploy to manipulate him into sharing information. She was simply doing what she enjoyed, delighting someone she loved with pleasure.

There had been uncomplicated conversation during the meal, talk of the weather and who had died, keeping him busy at the funeral home he ran, how Dick was thinking about buying a new golf club he had seen advertised in a magazine, and how her mashed potatoes were whipped especially light.

She had purchased a new dress at a winter sale at the mall, and while Dick ate a piece of the banana cream pie she had made over the weekend, she left her dessert and went to the bedroom, put on the new article of clothing, and modeled for him in the kitchen.

He had her turn around and step to the sink, then walk over to him so that he could feel the material; and he smiled at his wife and claimed that she appeared younger and thinner than she ever had and that if it was up to him, he'd marry her all over again as long as she wore that dress. Then he tilted his head back, exposing the front part of his neck, and Beatrice leaned down and kissed him just below his Adam's apple. In her mind, he had said exactly the right thing.

She returned to the bedroom and changed into what she had been wearing before, walked into the kitchen, and cleaned up the dinner dishes. Dick moved into the den and turned on the television while she finished her chores.

After nearly an hour she turned on the dishwasher, covered the pie with clear plastic wrap, put it in the refrigerator, and stood at the kitchen table, finally ready to ask the question.

She walked into the den and turned off the television. "I want to know," she said to him as he sat in his chair reading the paper, only minutes after the start of his favorite game show, "I want to know what is going on with your brother and his wife."

She had considered and honored what Louise had said to her. For days she had pondered the necessity of keeping certain secrets. She had agreed with her friend and had made a decision that she had no right to ask that her husband betray his family member's confidence and tell his wife what wasn't hers to know. She tried not to think of herself as being jealous of his sister-in-law.

She had not pestered him when he returned from the last trip to Winston. She did not snoop in his pockets or check the mileage on his car. She didn't needle him or inquire about the visit; she had remained steadfast and detached for more than eleven days. But then another day passed, and on the eleventh night of silence, the eleventh night of hearing nothing, knowing nothing, discussing nothing, she could not take it any longer.

"I want to know what is going on with your brother and his wife," she repeated when he did not put down his paper.

She stood just in front of the television, no more words spoken, and the sudden absence of any other noise in the room made her question and her questioning feel even more dramatic.

Dick folded the newspaper across his lap and studied his wife as she stood above him.

She was determined, her lips pursed in two tight lines, her eyes filled with an uneasy confidence, her chin high, her shoulders steady; and she just stood there, not quite close but near enough that she would not be turned away.

He took off his reading glasses and placed them on the small table next to his chair. He rolled his chin in his hand, still without saying a word. There was a long, drawn-out pause as she waited and as he thought of how to begin, how to speak to his wife's confusion and how to answer her question.

"O. T. and Jean are the only family members I have left," he said as if she didn't know it. "Nobody's heard from my brother Jolly in years. Mama passed ten years ago, and Daddy, well, you remember that story about him getting killed in that tractor accident."

Beatrice remained as she was, standing in front of Dick as he finally spoke of the truth. She already knew the strength of the relationship between Dick and his brother, even between Dick and his brother's wife, at first having mistaken her for his sister.

Dick began telling the story slowly and with great thought. He did it as if he had been waiting for her to ask, each word a stone on a path or a fingerprint at the scene, a clue to the mystery behind his silence.

"O. T. was more than just my brother. He was my best friend." Dick pulled his hand away from his face, settling in his chair. He set the story loose.

"He was the one who taught me how to pull and string tobacco and how to rewire the ignition system on the old Buick. He showed me how to fish and hunt, taught me everything I know about farming and money." Dick paused. "O. T. was the one who was always there for me." He thought about how much stronger his relationship was with his oldest brother than it was with the middle one.

Dick went on without prompting from his wife. "O. T. was—is," he corrected himself, "a good man, a really good man."

Beatrice nodded. She had liked her brother-in-law from the first time they met. She knew that Dick adored him.

"He fell in love and married Jean and brought her back to

the farm when I was just a little boy." He recalled how it was when the young couple moved in with them. "Jean wasn't very old herself, and I don't think Mama ever liked her, but me and Jolly did." Dick thought about his other brother and how he seemed especially smitten with the oldest son's young bride.

"O. T. went off to the war like all the men did. My brother Jolly didn't go because of something, I can't remember now, and, well, I was too young. We stayed on the farm and worked, and O. T. wrote us letters from all the places where he fought, and Jean would read them to me. She was like a big sister, but she worked as hard as any of us boys did." Dick smiled, thinking about how strong and capable the young woman was.

"A couple of years later, O. T. came home. They stayed with us for a while, and then they built their own place; and they seemed happy."

He paused, remembering the days from his past when family was everything to him. "I thought they were happy," he added.

"Years went by and finally Jean got pregnant. She really wanted a baby. They had been trying for a long time. O. T. seemed pleased." He thought about how his brother had called him with the news. Dick had been out of town, gone to a training session to be a funeral director. He remembered being surprised that O. T. had found out where he was staying.

He remembered how later they made a nursery, how O. T. built all the furniture and how they painted it yellow since they didn't know if it was a boy or a girl.

"Just before it was time something happened." Dick's voice cracked. "The baby died." He cleared his throat. "Before the little girl was born, she died inside Jean."

Beatrice was surprised to see the tear in her husband's eye.

He went on. "And it was bad for a while, harder on them than anybody imagined."

Beatrice dropped her head at this point, seeming a little sorry that she had demanded her husband speak of his family's private pain.

"People just didn't talk about babies dying back then. It was considered a private matter, and nobody ever asked any questions about that sort of thing." Dick continued to tell the story unhaltingly, as if it had been his idea to share it in the first place.

"O. T. mentioned it a time or two when we'd be together, that he worried because he wasn't sure Jean had dealt with the passing. He said she still kept the baby clothes and wouldn't talk about trying to have another child, that she had become withdrawn and didn't seem to care about anything." Dick paused, remembering the conversations.

"But then he'd soon change the subject and we'd talk about other things and I never thought much about it. I just assumed they would figure out how to put the past behind them and go on with their lives, the way all of us did in those days. I just assumed it was all going to be all right."

Beatrice slid her hands into the pockets of her sweatpants. She moved from side to side, steadying herself in her stance, feeling pity for her husband, who had never understood the quiet ways some people suffer.

"I guess it was much worse than anybody knew." He faced his wife like he thought she might answer. "Looking back now, I think maybe I should have been there for him more. I should have paid more attention to things, helped him and Jean out."

Beatrice did not respond.

"What I'm trying to say is that the marriage and the war and the baby, it was all a lot harder on Jean." Dick scratched his cheek and then rubbed his fingers across his eyes. "And O. T.," he added, "than anybody knew."

His brother had quit calling during that year after the death and he was never at home. Dick remembered how he thought something was wrong, something had changed, but he had never mentioned it. "I guess it just never got dealt with."

Beatrice nodded in sympathy.

"Anyway, he's not doing so well these days." Dick held out his right hand in front of him and appeared to study it, turning it from the front to the back.

Beatrice understood that her brother-in-law's condition had worsened in the last few months, but she wasn't following Dick's line of thinking. She didn't see the connection between the baby's death that happened decades ago and his present deteriorating health.

"And Jean, well, she's just having trouble with some things right now," Dick continued.

Beatrice didn't ask for an explanation since she assumed her husband still had more story to tell.

Dick hesitated at this point, then faced his wife. "There's a young woman who's been visiting him at the nursing home." Dick put his hand down on the arm of the chair. "A young woman Jean doesn't know."

Beatrice raised an eyebrow. Things weren't becoming clear, she thought, but at least they were becoming more interesting.

"Jean says the woman claims to be his daughter." Dick stopped and picked up his glasses. He folded them and stuck them in his shirt pocket.

Beatrice considered the shock of such news for a woman. She wondered how it must have been for Jean to discover such a thing about her husband.

"O. T., of course, doesn't recognize the woman, so he can't answer any questions, and Jean, well, she's just trying to figure things out." He remembered the phone call he had gotten when she first told him the news. "So, she asked me a month or so ago to help her sort through the legal situation now that this woman has shown up."

Beatrice dropped her eyes away from her husband. In the time of her silence, while respecting her husband's privacy, she had imagined all sorts of situations. She thought there could be financial concerns, that Jean couldn't pay the bills, that O. T. had spent all their money in one of his periods of confusion before he was institutionalized. She imagined that Jean was having family troubles or her own health problems or even that she was lonely and Dick was comforting her.

Beatrice had never considered that her husband, brother to a hero, was forced to face the disappointing knowledge that the person he had adored and worshiped for so long was not the immortal entity that he had set him up to be. O. T. was just a man, and he had made a mistake twenty years ago or more and fathered a child outside of his marriage. Beatrice wondered who was taking the news the hardest, O. T.'s wife or his brother.

She knelt down in front of her husband and lay her head in his lap. She tried to imagine what Jean was feeling, the betrayal of so long ago suddenly forced to the surface. She thought about O. T., a man confined to a bed in a strange place, confused and unforgiven, unable to explain what had happened. She thought about the young woman, boldly appearing at the doorstep of a father she had never known. She considered Dick and how he troubled himself into thinking he could have altered history, that he believed if he had been more of a brother to O. T., then perhaps he wouldn't have turned to somebody else, somebody who got pregnant. Finally, Beatrice began to understand the weight of knowing more than a person wanted to know.

She sat that way, kneeling before her husband, her arms wrapped around his waist, while dusk faded into darkness. She stayed in that position for almost an hour, just holding him, just thanking him for letting her know what had happened.

Before she finally stretched her legs and got up, before they changed the subject and talked of simpler things, before the lamp with the automatic switch turned on and gave light to the dark room, she wanted to tell her husband that what had happened to his brother really wasn't such a big deal, that it was Jean's problem and that he had no reason to be ashamed or embarrassed about it, that he couldn't have kept his brother from making the choices he made. She wanted to say that he had no reason to feel as if he couldn't talk about what had occurred, that people make mistakes and that O. T. was just like everybody else.

She wanted to say that Jean would work things out for herself, that she could manage this unfortunate situation on her own. But she didn't. Because sitting there near him, watching him sort through the disappointment and surprise of a brother's frailty, watching him struggle with how to help his sister-in-law, watching him think he was somehow responsible, she now understood that secrets are held for all sorts of reasons. A person doesn't always know why they can't speak of certain things.

They did not talk about it again that night. They completed a few tasks, read, paid a couple of bills, and finally separated to their bathrooms. They changed for bed, turned off the light, got into bed, and said good-night.

When they lay in the bed, Beatrice backed herself into her husband and, reaching behind her, pulled his arm around her, falling asleep with the gentle and regular puffs of his breath warming her neck.

When she got up to take her walk in the morning, he was still asleep, so she didn't wake him. She left the bed, the room, and the house quietly, and when she returned, he was gone. To his office, she supposed but considered that perhaps he had taken off to check on Jean.

"A secret's a funny thing," Beatrice said to herself as she sat at the table thinking about O. T. and Jean and the past that had revisited them. "A person can run away from lots of things, but the truth will always chase you down."

She sat for a minute and thought about calling Louise and telling her what she had learned. She wondered if she should talk to Margaret or maybe even Charlotte, but then she remembered how it was finally to hear and possess a secret, how long she had waited to have one of her own.

And now, suddenly, she realized that keeping a secret was harder than she had imagined, weightier, like a long and heavy board balanced across her shoulders. It was easier to carry than guilt or anger, but it was still, by itself, a difficult thing to maintain.

She remembered her talk with her friend and how Louise had told her that having secrets was usually not a good thing and that she should think of herself as lucky that she didn't have any. She remembered how the words had stung like a woman evicted from her home having to hear somebody complain about housework.

It had seemed condescending and patronizing, and it had angered Beatrice. But now, now that she had a secret, now that she understood her husband's need for silence and the lumbering nature of carrying a brother's burden, now that he had shared with her the real reason for his distraction and the sudden need to be gone, she realized that a secret was not such a lovely thing to have.

She was content, in a way, now that she knew, relieved that she didn't have to guess about it anymore, pleased that Dick had trusted her enough to tell her. But now knowing that Jean was having to face more than just her husband's imminent death and that Dick was having to deal with his hero's past mistakes, Beatrice wasn't sure that knowing the secret made her feel any better.

She reached out for Jessie's postcard again and placed it on the table before her. With her right index finger, she outlined the tiger and the cubs and the tree. Using small, delicate movements like an artist, she painted herself into the photograph of a mother and her babies, a family of creatures from God's own hand, and pondered the weight of betrayal and the sudden outing of truth.

"I guess having a secret is a bit like having your picture taken," Beatrice said out loud as if somebody was listening, "every one you keep or tell steals a little of your soul."

She put the card on top of the pile of mail, got up from the table, and slowly, like a woman suddenly grown old and wise, went back to the bathroom to take a shower.

Eight

THE PILOT NEWS

* A U N T * D O T'S * H E L P F U L * H I N T S *

Dear Aunt Dot,
Candle wax on the carpet. Unsightly stain. Any help will be appreciated.

Waned and Waxed

Dear Waned,
Try using a warm iron on brown paper over the stain. You may have to use some elbow grease, but this usually works!

You need to come to the church." That was all the voice on the other end of the phone said. Charlotte was still asleep when the call came in. She stumbled a bit with her reply. She felt herself being pulled away from a bus.

"Who is this?" she asked as she sat up in her bed, reaching for the clock. It was 7:15 A.M., Monday, her day off. She remained unclear, the dream of the bus and the strange old woman starting to pass beyond the edges of her mind.

It had been about her father again; this much she knew. He had been a player in her dreams at least once a week for the past few months. Sometimes his role carried the entire story, and sometimes he was just a bit actor, a face in a crowd, an unobtrusive presence in an otherwise crowded scene. But he had been always present and always a man bigger than life, his large size always noticeable.

For years she had nothing of him in her nighttime fantasies. Even when there were dreams of her mother and Serena, he was missing, unaccounted for, never represented. And when she woke and remembered the emotions of seeing her dead sister or encountering the blocked memories of her alcoholic mother, the daughter did not even miss her father, barely noticed his familial absence. But now, in the past year, in the months of structured therapy, he had suddenly emerged, a force with which to reckon, a memory to be recalled.

Marion had encouraged her to record the dreams, claiming that they bore important information about her relationship with her dad and the unfinished business of what they did and did not have. Charlotte agreed that these new dreams held clues of how she really felt, what she honestly remembered, but she had discovered that recording them was a difficult task to perform.

It was something she had to do just after waking because if she didn't jot the dream down right away, it quickly slipped out of her memory and was gone, just as if it had never happened. She'd feel a sense of having been visited, having almost remembered things, but if she didn't wake up and reach for a pad and paper to list the contents of the dream, she could hardly recall its existence. It was as if there was a part of herself that preferred them to stay shrouded in darkness, unleashed only in sleep.

She turned and saw the journal next to the phone and considered putting the caller on hold just so she could write down the dream she now clearly remembered but that would probably be gone in a few minutes. She was unsure what to do.

"Is this Charlotte Stewart?"

She did not reach for the book. "Yes," she answered, the images already starting to fade.

The dreams were merely images at first, a string of pictures flashing before her like pearls on a necklace. One by one they emerged, scenes from her childhood frozen and captured, long ago forgotten. The family sitting around the table at mealtime, the birthday cake placed before her sister's shining eyes, the group posed in song; the two of them, father and daughter, standing in front of an old car, the little girl shielding her eyes from the sun. Images of lost memories that were now beginning to tell stories as she slept.

Mostly when the dreams stretched into more than just flashbacks, they would be pieces of anticipatory events, slices of a life bent in waiting but squeezed into distraction. Sometimes in her dream she would be expecting news, confirmation of a proposal or arrangement, and other times she was waiting for a person to emerge, someone to meet her, an angel unveiled, or perhaps she herself was preparing to travel. She was, however, never able to receive the thing or the person for whom she waited, never able to leave, because there always seemed to be some task to complete, some activity in which to participate. And apparently, because of the distraction or activity, she had never, in the four or five weeks in which the images had turned into scenes or stories, ultimately found or uncovered or had revealed to her the thing for which she had waited. It had become a pattern of unfulfillment, and she was beginning to sense that her subconscious was simply mirroring for her what she knew all too clearly. The desire of her heart, the immeasurable longing, could never be satisfied.

In this dream, Charlotte remembered as she held the phone next to her ear, she is at a bus stop. She waits with a duffel bag filled with heavy items. She is not burdened by what she carries, but she is impeded by the weight and the awkwardness of having to balance the bag and its contents upon her back. There are others waiting with her, a couple of men, more women, some with bags and suitcases and some with nothing in their hands.

When the bus arrives and the door opens, everyone moves toward the front. Charlotte, as she peers through the windows of the bus, notices that it is her father driving. He is young and big, tall, the way she remembers him from early photographs and first recollections. He sits, filling up the entire driver's seat, his right hand on the door lever, his left on the large black steering wheel. They are big hands, hands of a working man, tan and callused. He never looks at the passengers, never sees his daughter. He doesn't seem perturbed or unhappy, just focused on the task at hand.

Charlotte feels nothing for her father, not surprise or anger or pleasure, and as the other people begin to get on board, Charlotte turns to see a lady sitting in front of the bus, on the bench. She is an old white woman with gnarled hands, small and bony, hardly the size of an adult. She wears a blue scarf on her head, and her clothes are wrinkled and unkempt. She seems, however, unbothered by how she appears and is polishing a silver candlestick like the kind at church, the tall ones that stand on the altar in the center of the chancel.

Charlotte is struck by the gleaming silver, the tarnish lifted and the shine reflecting in the light of the sun. And as in all the other dreams where she is pulled away from the task at hand, she is torn between staying at the bus stop and asking the woman to polish the items in her duffel bag and doing what is apparently intended and getting on board. Her father patiently waits as the other people hurry by her and step onto the bus. The young pastor is just opening her bag, the bus door still ajar, when the phone call interrupted her sleep and her dream.

"It's Grady, Charlotte," the voice not at all apologetic for waking the minister.

Charlotte cleared her throat, trying to pay attention to the conversation someone was seeking to have with her and trying to push the dream aside without forgetting it. She watched powerlessly as the pictures fled her mind. Grady Marks, she remembered, the deacon chairman, the lay leader of the church.

"What's wrong?" she asked.

"I think somebody broke into your office. The door was standing open. I came by to check on the heat because I wasn't sure it got turned off yesterday, and I noticed that it wasn't shut and locked." He waited to see if Charlotte was still listening.

"Did you call the police?" She got out of bed.

"No," he answered. "I thought I'd talk to you first."

Charlotte was surprised that he had not taken matters into his own hands, something the church leader was known to do, and called his buddies at the sheriff's office before he had contacted her. She knew that it was unlike him, and she wasn't sure whether this was a good sign or a bad one.

"I'll be right there." She hung up the phone and threw on some clothes and walked over to the church.

It took only a few minutes since the parsonage was next door. When she came in, Grady was sitting in the choir room, just across the hall from the pastor's office. When the door shut behind her, she heard his chair slide across the floor and he met her in the entryway.

"Did you go in?" she asked as she pushed the office door open.

He nodded his head and followed her as she walked in. "I

didn't touch anything, though, and I called you because you'd know better than anyone what was missing out of here."

She turned on the lights and looked around.

At first sight, nothing appeared to be out of place. Her desk was just like it was when she left yesterday after the worship service. The remaining bulletins were on the shelf by the door going into the outer office, and the communion set was exactly where she had placed it, on the corner of the small table positioned next to the window. The drawers of her desk were not open, and the phone and answering machine were in their usual places.

She moved her eyes slowly and attentively across the room. The plants were there; the curtains were still hanging; the bookends and the books had not been taken.

Grady walked into the other office. He switched on the light and checked the other door.

Charlotte continued taking inventory of the things in her office, noting that her pictures remained on the wall, supplies were on the desk, the clock was keeping the right time. She slowly paid attention to everything in the room, examining from side to side, up to down; and as she stopped to focus on the area around her chair she noticed that the CD player was missing.

She walked around the desk and scanned the area near the trash can. Grady came back to where Charlotte was. He stood just in the doorway that separated the pastor's office from the other room.

He watched her for a minute and then asked, "Anything gone?"

Charlotte didn't want to report the missing item just yet. She wasn't sure it was in fact missing and decided instead to hear what else the church member obviously wanted to say.

He seemed convinced there had been a break-in.

He waited, and when his pastor didn't respond, he glanced into the office behind him and then out the window next to Charlotte's desk and then without hesitation said, "I see that Vastine and Peggy's grandson is staying with them."

Charlotte faced the deacon. Suddenly she understood the reason for his concern and the early-morning call. She figured she'd play along. "He's been home two weeks. He was at church yesterday."

She waited to hear more of the older man's implications.

"Yeah, I saw him standing around here before service." Grady leaned against the frame of the door. He was wearing navy pants with a jacket that matched, a uniform for work, his name stitched in red and white just over a left breast pocket. A ball cap covered most of his forehead, and he lifted the brim a bit so that he could stare at his pastor eye-to-eye.

Charlotte didn't respond.

Grady threw his left leg across his right one. "He was in jail, is what I heard."

Charlotte was still quiet. She knew that the teenager's story would be shared among the church members, and she hadn't been sure how they would react. With such a lack of subtlety in Grady's conversation, she felt a sinking in her stomach at what had apparently already been discussed.

He folded his arms across his chest, heavy and dramatic, like he was lodging a complaint. "We have a history with that boy," is how he said it.

"A history?" Charlotte asked. She pushed her chair away from the desk a bit without losing eye contact with her parishioner.

"He stole some things from us the last time he stayed with Vastine and Peggy."

Charlotte rested her hands on the arms of her chair; she tried not to take a defensive position. She looked around some more, still trying to locate the CD player. She raised her eyebrows, waiting for more of the story that he seemed willing to tell.

"And he was how old then?" she asked innocently.

"Eight or nine, I don't remember," he replied.

"I heard he was more like six or seven." Charlotte remembered what Peggy had told her and corrected Grady in hopes that, once he was reminded of Lamont's young age when he was in Hope Springs before, reason might cast aside his unproved ideas of blame.

"Well, I don't recall how old he was; I just know that we had trouble then and now he's back and—"

Charlotte didn't let him finish. "And we have trouble now?" She phrased it in a question. "Grady, I don't see that anything is missing. I probably just didn't lock the door."

The deacon had a toothpick in his teeth, and he pushed it from one side of his mouth to the other.

"Does everything appear all right in the other office?" Charlotte remained at her desk.

Grady nodded, the toothpick still twirling between his teeth.

"Then I don't think we've got a problem." She paused. "Do we?"

The older man shook his head and studied his pastor. Charlotte could tell that he was contemplating saying more. She braced herself for what was coming.

"Well, the other men and I talked about it, and we agreed that somebody should keep an eye on him." He stuck his hands in the pockets of his jacket. His name lifted off his chest.

Charlotte felt herself turn red. Not only had there been discussion about Lamont's return to the community; a decision had been made about how he would be treated.

As his words settled upon the young minister, Charlotte realized that once again she had underestimated the malice and the harm that can be done in a church. She understood that Peggy's embarrassment and shame had as much to do with the reactions of her community to her grandson's criminal activities as they did with her serious considerations that she had been at fault. The DuVaughns had never spoken of their burden or concerns about Lamont because the Hope Springs church members had already made it clear that they would never welcome the boy back into their midst.

Charlotte felt a tightening in the back of her throat.

"Grady," she said as calmly as she could, "the DuVaughns

have their grandson staying with them because Peggy needs some help taking care of Vastine. Lamont was kind enough to move in with them and look after his grandfather." She sat straight up, rigid and undeterred. "You and I have been through a lot together," she added.

The older man narrowed his eyes at her.

"I have a great deal of respect for you and the work you do in this church." She did not falter. "But, Grady, that young man is a member of this community, a member of one of our families, and as long as I'm the pastor here, he will be treated with the utmost respect and hospitality." Charlotte surprised even herself with her confidence.

Grady was not changed. He reached up and effortlessly pulled the toothpick out of his mouth and pushed his tongue along the front of his teeth. He rocked a bit from side to side. "That boy's a thief. Everybody here knows that. And several of us believe he's dangerous. If you're so fired up to do the pastor thing, you ought to make sure he ain't stealing from Vastine and Peggy. They're the ones who need watching out after, not him."

He stuck the toothpick back in the corner of his mouth and readjusted his hat. "You weren't here when that boy made all his trouble; we were. And I'm here to make sure right from the start that none of that mess is going on at this church."

He put his hands in his pants pockets and jingled his keys. "Our welcome lasts just as long as his good behavior. If stuff starts getting missing around here, we're pressing charges."

He stared at Charlotte like he knew she was covering something. "And you can mark my words about that." He curled his lips around the toothpick and nodded like he was finished.

Charlotte did not move. "I thank you for your concern today, Grady. I'll check the heat and lock the doors behind me."

The man made a huffing sound like perhaps he would say more, but he didn't. He walked out of the office without even offering a good-bye.

When the back door slammed Charlotte ducked her head beneath the desk, trying once again to locate the CD player. She searched behind the trash can, next to the small table; she even got up and opened the cabinets, thinking that perhaps she had stuck it inside, on one of the shelves. It was definitely not in her office.

She recalled what Grady had said before his grand announcement about what he considered as his responsibility to protect the belongings of the church and remembered that Lamont had been standing outside her office just before church had started. When she saw him, she asked why he wasn't in the sanctuary, and he reported that he was going outside to smoke a cigarette before he joined the others. At the time Charlotte hadn't thought anything about it. But she knew that the missing item had been left beside her desk before the service.

She had played a CD for the choir director during Sunday school, an old gospel hymn that she thought the choir might want to learn for later in the spring. After playing the song, she had taken out the CD and given it to the music director and had put the player beside where she was sitting. Lamont had come around just about that time.

Charlotte got up from her chair and walked through the outer office into the sanctuary. She sat on the first pew, without turning on any lights. Even in the darkness she could see the drippings from the candle wax that had been spilled in front of the chancel steps during the Christmas Eve service two years before. No one had cleaned the stains.

The church was quiet, the way she preferred it, and she positioned herself way down in the seat, resting her neck against the top of the pew. She laid her hands in her lap and closed her eyes. She sat in the silence and thought about Peggy and Vastine and about Lamont, the young man who had returned to the church, stirring up gossip and nerves.

She wasn't sure if she should confront the boy about the missing CD player, go over to Peggy and Vastine's and make sure that he wasn't stealing from his grandparents, or just leave things alone, waiting until she heard from them.

She knew that it would be difficult for Peggy to admit if Lamont was stealing from them, and Charlotte understood that he could take everything from his grandparents before anyone else might hear about what had happened, leaving them in dire circumstances.

The minister placed her hands on top of her head and interlaced her fingers and remembered how Peggy had appeared when Lamont got out of the car and walked toward the house, having just come home from jail.

Peggy met them both at the porch, her face flushed and expectant. She had a dishtowel in her hands, and she waved it like a flag when she saw them. And then as the pastor and the teenager moved up the steps, the older woman jumped up and down. Jumped, Charlotte remembered, just as if her joy could not be contained, just as if she could not stand still, just as if this old woman had become young.

The grandmother was so eager and overwhelmed with emotion that after she grabbed Lamont and pulled him into herself, she led him in from the front door and straight into the bedroom where Vastine was resting, leaving Charlotte alone on the porch. The pastor had walked in behind them.

"Honey, look who's here!" she had said, her voice loud and unwavering.

Lamont, unhesitantly and with ease, had stepped beside the hospital bed and taken his grandfather's hand, "Hey, Pop," he had said and bent down to kiss the old man on the cheek.

Vastine had reached out and held him there, their faces touching until the teenager almost lost his balance and fell into the bed next to him.

"Whoa," he said jokingly, "you're about to pull me in there with you." But he was obviously touched by the joy of his family, by the homecoming and welcome he had received.

Charlotte had watched from the hallway, overcome by what she had seen. She knew that the chances that the young man would stay clean and sober and out of trouble were very slim. She understood that because of his history and recklessness, because of his addiction, which had apparently begun at an early age, the odds were that he was going to steal everything his grandparents owned, maybe even take and use the old man's medications. But, standing in her parishioners' house, a visitor invited into intimacy, she also knew what she had seen, trusted what she had witnessed.

Lamont had been welcomed home, received in love, and it had been for Charlotte the most literal and clear demonstration of a Bible story that she had heard all of her life, the story of the prodigal son, the story of an unconditionally loving father.

The pastor remembered the text from the Gospel of Luke, the parable Jesus told about a young man who asked his father for his inheritance and then took the money and spent it wildly. He wasted all that he had, ultimately finding himself with nothing, hungry and alone, standing in a pig lot, eating the slop reserved for the swine. In that moment of desperation and self-realization, the young man decided to go home and ask to be his father's servant. And when he was almost at his house, the father, who had waited and watched every day for his son's return, ran to meet the estranged child, greeted him with a kiss and undeserved mercy, and threw a party for him in honor of his homecoming.

It was, Jesus had said to his followers, a story about celebrating that one who had once been lost, now having been found. It was, in the young pastor's mind, the complete and defining story of what she understood the gospel to be about. It was this story that called her to be a Christian. It was also, however, this story that made her ashamed to be one.

Charlotte remembered that the other character in this Jesus story about God's mercy and love was not so happy about the boy's return, not so welcoming, not so merciful. And Charlotte was beginning to understand more and more clearly that the older brother who had stayed at home and worked in the fields, the one who had obeyed the rules and lived an honorable life, the one who did not spend his father's money and would not celebrate his brother's return, was usually the one sitting in church every Sunday, the one who served on the deacon board, and the one who was determined to press charges and punish a teenage thief.

Charlotte lay down on the pew and rubbed her fingers across her eyes. She curled her legs beneath her and placed her hands under her head like a pillow. She thought about the situation with Peggy and Vastine and truly didn't know what should be her place in the family dilemma. She was unsure of her pastoral responsibility to the DuVaughns or to the other parishioners, and she was disappointed that, since the CD player was missing, fears about Lamont's behavior might be realized. But these were not the things that troubled her most.

She turned on her back and looked up at the ceiling of the sanctuary. The heater switched on, and the soft motor breathed warmth into the large room. What troubled the young pastor the most as she rested in her place of worship, pulled out of bed by the panic of the church's most prominent leader, was that she recognized that she was working in a place, serving a people, who might never understand how a sinner gets welcomed home.

She closed her eyes, feeling heavy and grave, painfully aware of what she had always suspected. When Jesus told the story that made some people weep with joy at how a father can love, he had also reminded them that most religious people don't.

Older brothers, who live their narrow lives hiding in church, disabled by bitterness, slice and dispense mercy like small, cheap cuts of meat. And the minister, awakened and alone and dreamless, lay in the sanctuary troubled because she understood they expected their pastor to do the same.

Nine

* A U N T * D O T ' S * H E L P F U L * H I N T S *

Dear Aunt Dot,
I got chocolate on my favorite dress. Should I just take it to the cleaners or should I try to get it out myself?

Chocoholic

Dear Chocoholic,
Your dry cleaner should be able to handle the stain. Just make sure to make them aware of it when you take your dress in. Since this is an item you have cleaned profession-ally, the stain should come out easily. For other chocolate spills, you can try a mixture of 1/4 cup mineral oil to 2 cups dry-cleaning solvent. Blot with this after rinsing in cold water. Then flush with more of the solvent. And finally, wash normally. Hopefully you can still eat your cake with-out having to wear it!

*E*xcuse me, but are you finished with the dryer?" Lana stood in front of the old man who was reading the newspaper as he sat in the chair by the window.

"I'm sorry, what?" he asked as he lowered the paper. He lifted his face, answering the young woman.

"The dryer," she answered. "It's finished its cycle, and it's the only one not being used."

She had been watching when the old man took his clothes out of the washer and placed them in the large machine. She had noticed the time and assumed that he should be finished when she would need to move her clothes over. All of the other dryers were being used by the staff at the cleaners, a couple of college students, and one middle-aged Hispanic woman who kept running next door to a convenience store trying to get change.

The only opportunity Lana had to finish her clothes without waiting was to be able to use the appliance that the old man had gotten to first. She glanced around the Laundromat, hoping that the other woman hadn't returned from the store yet. She had been watching for the old man's clothes to finish as well since she still had one more load to dry.

"Oh," the man responded. "Are my clothes done already?" He checked his watch and got up from his seat.

Lana walked behind him as he headed toward the dryer, opened the door, and reached inside.

"These things are always the problem." He lifted out a

towel, still heavy and damp. He shook his head apologetically. "You know, I think they need some more time."

And he pulled out three quarters from his pocket and placed them in the coin slot in the machine. "I'm sorry," he said as he turned to Lana, "but I do thank you for letting me know that my time was up." And he patted the young woman on her head as if she was a child.

Lana turned up her lips, trying to fake a smile, but she frowned and rolled her eyes as soon as the old man walked away, returning to his seat. She moved to the washer and began pulling out her wet clothes and dropping them in the laundry basket.

Lana hated having to come to the Laundromat. She felt destitute and undignified being there. It was beneath her. Yet, in spite of how it made her feel to display her dirty laundry in front of strangers, she preferred that to having to sit with her mother for the entire morning. Lana knew she'd rather feel poor than indebted, something she always felt when she was around her family.

She had told Wallace that the washer at the house was making some strange noises not long after his grandparents had left for their trip. She had planned to call somebody to come fix it over a week ago. She had forgotten, and the last time she washed clothes, smoke poured from the back of the appliance and it shut off just before the final spin cycle.

They had to wring out every piece of clothing by hand and use a large plastic pitcher to remove all of the water from inside the machine. The pantry flooded, and the repairman who came the next day said that the machine was beyond simple maintenance. It was so old and used that it was less expensive just to buy a new one than to fix the one Wallace's grandparents had.

"Great," she said as she remembered the man's report. "How can we pay for that?" she asked herself.

Lana stood in front of the row of washers, pulling out Hope's T-shirts and play clothes, checking to make sure the stains from candy and Kool-Aid had come out. She held up the clothes, examining them inside and out, satisfied that the simple wash had gotten the stains clean.

She pulled out her jeans and baby bibs, towels and her family's underwear, and surprised even herself when suddenly she began to cry. She was late for work, so broke that she didn't have money for lunch, Hope was sick again with another virus, and she was still caught in a web of deceit and uncertainty.

She had tried finally to talk to her husband a few nights earlier, thinking that he might know how to help her, that she might be able to explain, but then the baby had spiked a fever and Wallace had to take an extra shift at work and she hadn't known where she would find the right words anyway. She continued to manage things, but she realized she was nearing the end.

"I'd forgotten how much messy laundry children make." The voice was smooth and familiar and coming from behind Lana.

She quickly wiped her eyes and turned around. Nadine was standing right in front of her.

"Yeah, there's always dirty clothes with a baby." Lana slid back her hair and adjusted her ponytail.

Nadine could tell that Lana had been crying but she decided not to comment about it right away. She had a load of clothes she was washing for a customer and a load that needed to be folded. She set down the basket with the clean clothes beside her feet and opened the top of the washer beside Lana, placing a key in a slot just above the lever that took coins.

"Your machine busted?" she asked as she poured the detergent inside.

Lana nodded. "Last week," she replied.

"Wouldn't your grandmother, the famous Aunt Dot, let you use hers?" Nadine smiled as she asked the question.

"Not without explaining every stain on every piece of clothing and what will and will not work to get it out," Lana answered, remembering how her grandmother was about laundry.

"Well, then, I'm glad you're here." Nadine dropped the dirty clothes into the machine.

"Yeah, but I hate to have to tell Mrs. Jenkins when she gets home that we broke her washer." Lana continued pulling out her wet clothes and placing them in her basket.

"That's right. They get back next week, don't they?"

Jessie had spoken about the African trip at church, asking for prayers during the worship service before they left, a safe journey and God's guidance for their travels.

"Have you heard from them?" Nadine asked. "Have they had a good time?" She dropped the laundry into the machine and shut the lid.

"They call every couple of days." Lana felt around inside the machine, making sure she had gotten all the clothes. "They've enjoyed themselves, I think." She tried to see if any dryer had become available. Nothing had changed.

"That must be great to be able to visit other places like that," Nadine responded. She turned the knob to the appropriate setting and pulled it out to start the wash cycle. "I'd love to go that far away."

Lana turned around and leaned against the washing machine. She looked out the window at the diner across the street, the place where she and Roger had met for lunch a few times.

"Yeah, I'd like to leave here, go somewhere far away, but with a baby, well, there isn't much going anywhere with a baby." Then she remembered Nadine's situation, the absence of little Brittany suddenly an obvious hole between the two women.

"I'm sorry," she said awkwardly as Nadine averted her eyes and stared down at the clothes near her feet. "I'm always doing that. Lately it seems that I can't say the thing that needs to get said, and yet I always manage to say the things that shouldn't."

"It's okay," Nadine answered, facing Lana. "I'm not so messed up anymore that mothers can't talk about their children in front of me." Nadine put the basket of clean clothes on top of the machine on the other side of her and turned around and placed her hands on the washer behind her, gently lifting herself to sit on top of the machine.

Lana nodded and followed her lead, and they sat on the washers side by side.

"It's taken a long time, but I'm learning how to be alone again." Nadine pulled out a laundry bag from the bottom of the basket and placed it behind her. "I suppose there are worse things than that."

Lana glanced up at the ceiling. "What?" she asked, noticing the dark water stains and the dirty light fixtures. "You mean worse than being alone?"

Nadine nodded. "Yep," she replied. "I expect there are lots of folks in huge families, surrounded by people all the time, who are more lonesome or unhappy than those of us by ourselves."

The washer quickly switched to the next cycle, and Nadine shifted a bit as the machine began to bounce. "I see a lot of unhappy people in here." She picked out some of the clean clothes and began to fold them. "Women with so much laundry that it takes them all day to wash."

Lana thought about the other woman she had seen in the Laundromat, wondering where she had gone. She thought about women with more than one child, women having to raise their children without any help. She knew her problems felt insurmountable but she had always known she would have somebody to help her take care of the baby.

"They seem so miserable, so broken down." Nadine paused. "Stuck in some life they didn't choose." She thought about all the people she had seen in the year she had been working at the Laundromat. She had learned a lot about life being there. She swung her body around and pulled the basket near her. She thought about her work.

Nadine hadn't been interested in a job when she got the one at the cleaners. She was only trying to get directions to the university when she stopped at the Laundromat. Mrs. Howard was working at the time. She was round and plump, a stout woman and part owner of the cleaners. She had been trying for over six months to find somebody to work the early shift so that she could spend more time taking care of her mother at a nearby nursing home.

She liked the looks of Nadine, she said. Thought she would make a fine employee. And before the young woman even considered taking a job, Mrs. Howard had shown her everything in the shop, explained to her about how the machines work, how tickets were written up, and how much starch to use when pressing to get a crisp snap in shirts.

She gave Nadine a set of keys within that first hour, without even checking her references or finding out where she lived. "I have a knack for ironing pleats, getting out stains, and reading people," she said as Nadine filled out the tax forms. "You've got a good heart. I could really use that around here."

And Nadine was so taken by the woman's kindness, by the anonymity in the relationship, and by the thoughts of keeping things clean, she had agreed. She started working the very next day.

Within three months she was given a raise and the title of

Laundromat manager. With her classes in social work and the time she spent washing and ironing and arranging freshly pressed clothes in plastic wrap, she had found her niche.

"Sometimes," Nadine said to Lana, "I think of the Laundromat as a metaphor for what we all need, some place where we walk in desperate and soiled, find the right solution, the right mixture of soap and water, the right ingredient to break down whatever stains we have, the right machine." She matched a pair of socks, held them together, and folded them inside each other. "And we cleanse and rinse, tumble dry, and walk out sorted and relieved. Clean," she added while Lana studied her movements, listened to her talk. She smiled and continued. "But that's pretty stupid since nothing in life is ever that tidy. There ain't a place to go and get all that for seventy-five cents." She dropped the socks in the basket and reached in for more clothes. "What about you?" she asked the younger woman.

Lana was confused.

"You ever feel like laundry?" Nadine rarely made time for idle conversation since her daughter's death. She had learned if something was on her mind it was better just to go ahead and speak it. This level of forthrightness sometimes unnerved those around her. Her mother claimed she had gotten too straightforward for people, but she didn't care. Life was short and costly. Not enough time for silly games of useless dialogue.

Lana kept her focus straight ahead. She didn't know how to respond. In the first place, she wasn't sure exactly how she did feel, and in the second place, she had not said such things out loud to anybody. She remembered the conversation with Margaret Peele, but she hadn't admitted anything then. She had only listened.

Lana closed her eyes. She knew she needed to talk to somebody. She knew the affair was meaningless, that she was heading to a place of no return.

Wallace had begun to appear so helpless around his wife that the sloping way he walked and the careful way he spoke when he was home only made her feel more desperate. She wasn't sure whether she was going to explode, the pieces of her jumbled heart flying out from inside her and landing, like ashes, upon the skin of everyone she loved, or whether she was simply going to drift away, fade inside herself, like the women in the Laundromat whose self-worth and happiness seemed as empty and narrow as the slots on the machines where coins were dropped in and fell through.

"I'm seeing another man," the young woman quickly confessed.

Nadine didn't respond. The machine shook beneath her, and she kept taking out articles of clothing from the basket, folding them, and placing them on the washer beside her.

"I don't love him, though," Lana added. "I don't know why I keep going to him." It felt surprisingly good to say it out loud. "It's almost as if I hope I'll get caught." The words fell out as strangers walked around the two women, washing and drying and folding their clothes. Lana was shocked at the ease with which she spoke of her trouble. It had taken so very little to get her to talk.

"I met him at school. He's a teacher." She opened and closed her hands as they rested in her lap. "I'm thinking of leaving Wallace and Hope." She pulled at the front of her pants. "I think they'd be better off without me. I think I don't know how to be a wife and a mother. I think I've made a mistake."

Lana thought about the letter she had written and kept in her purse, the letter so unlike the one Jessie had written to Wallace and left on the kitchen table.

She had penned it three days earlier. She had even filled her suitcase, Roger having promised to take her in. She had written instructions about Hope's schedule and care, what time she took a nap, which doll was her favorite, and how to stop her from crying.

Wallace hadn't noticed the empty place in the closet, the extra room in the dresser drawers, the clean shelf in the medicine cabinet. Or, she thought, if he has noticed he hasn't objected. And she considered this even more reason to leave. She was only waiting for the right time.

Yesterday was no good because Hope was still sick and the repairman was coming and somebody needed to be there to let him in the house. Today was no better since laundry needed to be done. Tomorrow might not work since there was nobody to watch the baby, so she wasn't sure when it was that she would break up her home, that everything would change.

There was a pause between Lana and Nadine as the missing middle-aged woman opened the door and came back into the Laundromat. Her face was tight and red, her hair loose and falling in her eyes. She walked over to Nadine and held out a rumpled piece of Mexican currency. Nadine seemed to recognize it, but she only shook her head.

"Cambio," the woman said with a heavy accent. "Necesito cambio."

Nadine pointed to the sign written in Spanish that said only U.S. dollars were accepted, but the woman kept pushing the bill in front of the employee and saying, "Cambio." She was becoming frantic, her voice loud and strained. "Cambio," she said again, her hair flying around her.

"Okay, okay," Nadine responded. She got up from her seat, taking the Mexican bill with her, and went to the cash drawer behind the counter. Everyone in the Laundromat knew it was against the rules for the workers to exchange Mexican money, but they all looked away without concern. Nadine returned to the woman and gave her more than a handful of quarters. The woman took the money and held onto Nadine's hand in a display of gratitude.

"Gracias," she kept saying over and over. "Thank you." Then she moved away from the two women and placed the coins in the stopped dryers to pay for another cycle for her laundry.

Nadine jumped on the washer, taking her seat again. She pulled out a man's shirt from the basket. She pressed her hand down the center of it and folded it in a small ordered square.

"She comes in here every three weeks, never has U.S. money." She turned toward the woman who needed change. "I guess she's using up all of her savings she brought with her when she came."

Lana studied the woman. She wasn't that old, maybe midthirties. She had three dryers going and another load of laundry still waiting to be done. She rubbed the remaining quarters between her fingers with a faraway look in her eyes, uncontained sadness.

Nadine finished folding the clothes and began sorting them by size. She jumped down and was standing near Lana, beneath her young friend. "When I tried to kill myself, I don't think I really wanted to die."

She placed the large pieces of clothing in one pile and the smaller ones in another. Lana didn't speak.

"I mean, I did want to die because I was so—Jesus—" she stopped. "So lost." She fingered the lace on a child's blouse. "But I also wanted to live because I figured that the worst punishment I could get was in staying alive."

Nadine pulled out the small blouse and held it up. It was pink with white polka dots and a thin piece of white lace around the neckline and cuffs.

She went on. "I knew that dying was the easy thing, the least difficult thing, and part of me craved that." She folded the little shirt, placing it on top of the pile, and looked up at Lana. "I mean, there was a part of me that just wanted to be done with everything, just be finished. And as weird as it seems, that may have been the healthiest part of me at the time." She talked as if she was only beginning to understand things for herself.

"I know it sounds weird, I'm sure, to think that the portion of my mind that everybody thought was the sickest was really the fragment designed to save me." She stopped folding and considered what she was saying.

"But you see, it seems to me that the part of me that wanted to live, the elements of my psyche or spirit or whatever it was that wanted me alive, saw my life only as a punishment, like it was some exercise of torture for a prisoner of war who was going to die anyway. It wasn't the inclination to stay alive that should have been trusted; that tendency was tainted by guilt and the need to punish. It was the inclination to die that saved me, the tendency to release myself from all the entanglements of Brittany's death, the desperation to be delivered and the idea that I deserved it. That was the part to be honored."

She reached for the laundry bag and opened it. "I mean, I don't think trying to commit suicide was the clearest decision of health, but I do think that the motives behind it were more healthy than the motives behind staying alive were."

Lana wasn't sure how to respond.

Nadine continued. "I guess what I'm trying to say is that sometimes we make choices that on the outside everybody thinks they know what they mean, that they're self-destructive or sinful or hurtful." She faced the younger woman. "But the truth is, they're just choices to keep people, maybe even ourselves, from seeing the real problem, the real reason we're self-destructive in the first place." She turned away and arranged the clothes in the laundry bag, smoothing them down as she put them in article by article.

"My choices to attempt suicide and to do drugs seemed like sorrow to everybody who knew me. Everybody just assumed they were choices of grief. 'Childless mother buckles under her bereavement.'" She said the last sentence like it was a newspaper headline, bold and heavy. "But nobody had a clue of how poisoned I was. Everyone, including me, underestimated the guilt." She pushed the clothes down into the bag. She hesitated.

"I just know that there's always more in a person's life than what you see; situations are always messier than what you think. It's like walking into a house. It may be all neat in the front room, a wide open space dusted and swept, and you may think it's a clean place." She tugged at the sides of the bag. "But until you've walked into all the rooms, you don't have a clue as to what you're dealing with. And there's something else," she added as she yanked the cord at the top of the laundry bag, pulling it taut. "Everybody's got a little dirt somewhere. You may feel like you're the only one with trouble, the only one trying to hide a mess, but the truth is, we all got a few stains. Trust me, there ain't nobody spotless." She tied the two ends of the laundry bag cord, making a giant bow. Just at that moment the washer in front of her stopped. Lana watched as Nadine opened the lid and placed the contents into the basket that she had dropped at her feet.

The old man, who had been sitting by the window, had left his place and moved over to the dryer. He was pulling out his clothes when he lifted his chin at Lana as a sign that he was finished. She jumped down from her perch, and she and Nadine walked over toward that side of the Laundromat, where the dryers stood side by side against the wall.

"Don't they smell good?" the man asked as he held up a towel to Lana's face.

She was surprised at his request, but she dropped her face into the towel, smelling it.

"My wife used to put fabric softener in the wash, but now it's already included in the detergent," he said as he began pulling his clothes out of the dryer. "She'd have liked that," he said. "The most important thing to her was not how the laundry looked but how it smelled. That's how you tell clothes are clean," he added.

Lana lifted her eyebrows at Nadine, who was busy checking the loads that the other employee had placed in the dryers. Two appliances were being emptied out. The woman who had needed change quickly threw her clothes in the first one available and dropped her coins in the slot and turned the dryer on. She returned to where she had been waiting. She was ironing men's shirts near the back, where customers could press and starch their clothes free of charge.

"There, it's all yours." And the old man took his armful of

clean laundry, dropped it in his basket, and headed out the door. He was humming some church song.

Lana threw her clothes in and started the dryer. She would need to call the office and tell them she would be late. She searched around for a phone and saw one near the vending machines. She turned to go in that direction, and when she glanced out the window, noticing the diner across the street, she saw Roger coming out with a young woman. A student, Lana thought, and was surprised not to feel anything at what she saw.

She watched them as he held open the door, his eyes following the slender line of her body, the easy way she let him, and Lana was not angry. She simply observed, unattached, uninvolved.

He reached his arm around her; and the young, unknown woman sidled into the man. She opened for him like a flower. Lana turned away when they walked behind the diner, to his car parked on the side street. She went over, picked up the phone, and dialed her place of employment.

"Hey, Claudia," she said to the other secretary in the front office of the bank where they worked. "The baby's sick again." She swallowed, unsure of why she felt so calm. "I'm going to have to take her to the doctor."

Then there was a brief exchange, including an apology, and she hung up the phone. Nadine had moved around her and was standing behind the counter. She had heard the conversation but asked nothing. She bent down and got some change out of her wallet and selected two candy bars from the vending machine, offering one to Lana. She didn't say anything to the young wife and mother.

Lana started to explain, but instead she just took one of the chocolate bars, opened the wrapper, and headed back to the dryers. She jumped up and sat on the last washer, her legs dangling over the side.

Nadine came up behind her. She sat on the same machine, facing the front. "What are you going to do?" she finally asked.

Lana shrugged her shoulders. She watched as her clothes spun and twisted, bumping from end to end, side to side, falling and tumbling over themselves, changing before her eyes.

She thought of them as her indescribable feelings, the unspoiled love for her daughter, whom she knew she would never forgive herself for leaving, the tenderness she felt for Wallace, and the shame of the carelessness with which she had treated their marriage. Over and over, side to side, the love and the unworthiness and the longing and the disappointment bumped and collided and fell.

A piece of chocolate spilled onto her shirt. When she reached down to wipe it off, it smeared, causing a small blemish just on the left side of her chest. She dabbed at it a bit and then turned to Nadine. "You got anything for this?"

The other woman jumped from her seat and moved around until she was standing right in front of Lana. She lifted up her friend's shirt a bit from the bottom to study the chocolate spill. "I've got just the thing for the stain on the outside." She stared at the younger woman. "But if there's more than that, you'll need to talk to somebody else. I just clean the clothes."

And Nadine turned and disappeared into the office, leaving Lana alone with her choices and the pieces of her heart.

Ten

* A U N T * D O T'S * H E L P F U L * H I N T S *

Dear Aunt Dot,
Any suggestions for tea stains?

Tea for Two

Dear Tea,
*For a washable article of clothing, try a soaking solution of
$\frac{1}{2}$ quart warm water with a little of your detergent and a
small bit of vinegar; flush with water. If it is a nonwashable
article, try rinsing first with cool water and then dab with a
small amount of vinegar; blot with a clean towel. Hopefully
the only spot of tea you'll be left with is the one still in the
cup!*

I t tastes a little like cinnamon." Louise took the first sip of
Kenyan tea that Jessie had brought back and was serving
to the women.

"Yes, there's cinnamon in it," Jessie responded as she walked into the den with a tray of English biscuits.

"What's it called again?" Beatrice asked as she smelled the top of her cup.

"Masala," Jessie answered. "It has cinnamon, cardamom, ginger, cloves, and black pepper."

"Black pepper?" Margaret asked. "I've never heard of putting black pepper in tea." She took one of the cookies and sampled it.

"That's what's interesting," Jessie responded as she sat down next to Louise, the tray placed in the center of the coffee table, the stack of photographs next to her feet. "I remember my grandmother putting pepper in tea. She used both black and red, claimed it had healing properties." She picked up her cup and took a sip. "It's an African custom."

Charlotte tasted the liquid. It was sweet and thick, almost medicinal. It coated her tongue.

"Here, put some milk in it." Jessie reached over the table and gave Beatrice the cream pitcher.

Beatrice poured a little milk into her tea and took a swallow. She lifted her eyebrows as she brought the cup down to the saucer sitting in her lap. "So rich," she reported. "Like that tea you get at the buffet at the Indian restaurant."

Jessie nodded. "Yes, there are some of the same spices in both teas. I think it's the cloves that are the most noticeable."

All the women took another sip, analyzing the tastes.

"So, tell us all about it." Louise sat back in the sofa. "Was it everything you hoped?"

"More." Jessie answered, picking up the first group of photographs. "It was like," she stopped to think, "it was like some dream or the final leg of a pilgrimage." She laid the photographs in her lap and took another sip. "It was a little like going home."

The other women listened without comment. Beatrice remembered the postcard she had received and her thoughts about Tennessee.

"Except it wasn't exactly like that because I've never thought of myself as African. And it was real obvious that we were different from the people there. But," she opened the envelope and pulled out the pictures. She looked at the first one, a shot of the village market. "There was just this sense of familiarity in the place, like part of me knew it."

"Déjà vu!" Beatrice replied. "Lots of people get it when they go somewhere. It's an ordinary phenomenon."

Louise turned toward her friend. "I don't think this is what Jessie is talking about. It's Africa, Beatrice. Africa?" She said the last word as a question, trying to push her friend along to understanding.

"Oh," Beatrice responded, staring down into her cup of tea. She crossed her eyebrows in confusion.

"No, Lou, it was sort of like déjà vu, only deeper somehow."

"I think I'd feel that way about Ireland." Margaret wiped the crumbs off her mouth with a napkin. "My mother's mother was Irish." As she named her, she thought of her grandmother, the distant memories that had never seemed to fade.

"I feel that way when I look at pictures of the Southwest, not the low desert so much as the high one." Charlotte sat up in her seat. "New Mexico, mostly."

Jessie faced her pastor. "Are your people from there?" she asked.

"I don't know. I don't think so," she answered as she began tracing back her family's roots in her mind. "When I see a picture or read a story from there, there's just something about the way I feel, down deep, like in my bones, that somehow makes me think that's where I began." She bit into a cookie.

"Could be a past life thing," Beatrice said as she reached across the table for more milk. She thought about her recent readings of people who had realized their past lives, noting that they kept finding themselves repeating things as if their spirits were trying to get something right.

She thought about her husband's brother and sister-in-law, the secret now out between them. She wondered if this unannounced woman, a new daughter, was some karmic connection to the dead daughter, wondered if all of it was somehow related to a past life experience for one of them.

"You know, I never believed that stuff until this trip. I only thought a person carried around the genes of their parents, maybe the grandparents, but when I walked along those streets or when we drove out into the plains, I felt like I had a hundred family members or more watching from inside me." She passed the group of photographs to Louise. "It was strange."

"Were the native people nice to you and James?" Louise

examined the pictures and then passed them on to Margaret, who was sitting beside her.

"Some of them were. Some weren't." Jessie picked up another stack and began flipping through them. "The connection wasn't so much with the people as it was with the land." She gave that stack to Charlotte, who was sitting across from her.

"Well, what all did you do?" Margaret asked.

"Everything we planned."

The women passed along the photographs, making comments about the sights, the beauty of the area, and the serene looks on the faces of their friend and her husband.

"We shopped, of course." She got up and brought in a cloth bag with souvenirs in it. She began handing out gifts. "Mostly wood carvings, some soapstone figures, a few textile pieces."

She handed Charlotte a statue, a large brown- and gold-faced woman connected to a base with five rings of bright colors painted around the bottom of the sculpture.

Charlotte held it and ran her fingers across it. The stone was smooth and heavy, the colors deep and vibrant. She faced Jessie, her expression a question mark.

"I bought it because she reminded me of you."

The other women studied the object in their pastor's hands.

"Big headed?" Beatrice asked as a joke.

Charlotte smiled.

"No," Jessie answered. "Strong with large eyes."

The minister studied the gift.

"You see more than you let on."

Charlotte kept her face down as she remembered her recent discussion with Peggy DuVaughn. The woman had not mentioned anything about Lamont or the people at church, but Charlotte had been able to tell that she had felt the animosity toward her grandson. Charlotte had wanted to apologize for the church members' behavior, but she hadn't known how. So they had muddled on in conversation without purpose or comfort.

"What's this?" Beatrice asked.

"It's a scarf," Jessie answered as she walked behind her friend and tied the piece of brightly colored fabric around her head. Beatrice sat up, able to see herself in the window behind the sofa. She turned her head from side to side, admiring herself. "I look like a queen!" she responded.

"Exactly," said Jessie.

Margaret pulled out tiny black elephants from a small paper bag. There were twelve of them, some larger than the others. She placed them on the table in front of her.

"It's a calendar," Jessie said to Margaret. She knelt down in front of her and placed the elephants in a straight line. "You keep them turned to the front until the month passes, then you turn them this way, one elephant for every month." And she began facing the elephants toward the wall. "I figured you have the deepest appreciation of time of all of us."

Margaret smiled and continued spinning the elephants so that they were all facing forward.

Louise was the last one to unwrap her gift. It was a small basket made from long, thick blades of yellow grass. A small woven lid rested on top.

"It's a replica of the ones the African women carry on their heads." Jessie took her seat. "You've always amazed me with what you keep balanced in here and in here." She pointed to her chest and her head.

Louise turned the basket over in her hands. The strands of yellow and green grass were perfectly woven inside each other, a melding of strength and beauty. "Thank you," she said.

There was a moment of silence as the women admired the gifts Jessie had brought them, each of them satisfied that she had handpicked the pieces, each of them enjoying the thought that their personalities had been considered and honored in their friend's purchases.

Charlotte put down her statue and picked up the pictures she had been examining and then turned to Jessie. She decided to ask the question. "Did you ever figure out what worried you so much, what caused your premonition?"

Jessie reached for a cookie, took a few bites, and then picked up her tea and drank the last of what she had poured for herself. She stared into the empty cup, trying to find the words to explain what she had asked herself almost daily for the month before they traveled.

She thought of how she felt when she left, burdened and fearful, how she almost canceled the trip, how James had constantly given her reassurances, but how they had not been enough to satisfy her.

"Yes," she answered Charlotte. "I finally figured it out." She dusted her lap, dropping small pieces of cookie onto the floor.

"At first, I thought it was going to have something to do with the two of us, that we'd be in a wreck or something." She eased back in her chair, remembering how frightened she had been on the plane. "And then it became clear that it was something here, something at home."

Margaret faced away from her friend and placed the elephants in a longer line, turning some toward the wall, pretending months had passed, wondering what Lana had decided.

Jessie answered Charlotte. "When we landed in Nairobi, as soon as we stepped off the plane and the hot, wet wind blew into us, the dust from the patch of land near the airport settling upon my lips and eyelids, I was okay. My spirit settled, my mind was focused, and my heart soared." She dropped her hands beside her. "I knew when we arrived and I placed my feet upon the brown earth that something old was new, that it was the beginning of something I had wanted for a very long time. That it was a new day, a bright, clean new day."

Charlotte kept her eyes on Jessie, remembering how Joyce would talk about starting over.

"It's strange, I know, but I had a sense that ultimately whatever was going to happen was going to happen whether I was here or not, that I couldn't control the fates of those I love. And that sometimes the best way to get clear, the best way to find peace, is to pay attention to your own longings, listen to your own pulse."

Charlotte turned away.

"I know that Lana and Wallace are having trouble," Jessie said matter-of-factly. She faced Margaret, who lowered her eyes. "I know that marriage is tenuous at best."

Beatrice thought of Dick and the secret they now shared together.

"I know that good health is a blessing and not a guarantee."

Margaret nodded without lifting her head.

"That love, like grief, can never be measured." She eyed Louise, who slid her fingers around the top of her basket and smiled.

"And that a woman's got to make her own way, figure out her own ideas, find her own measure of mercy."

Charlotte thought of the members of her church and the cold, empty place in her spirit.

"And then, clear head or premonition, a woman's got to go find things out for herself."

Jessie glanced around at the women who made her strong.

"But that's not really the truth," she said. "None of those things were really what had me troubled."

Charlotte set her eyes on Jessie, waiting for more.

"I didn't want to go to Africa because I was afraid that I would come home and blame you because of what my ancestors suffered."

The other women were bewildered, unprepared for what Jessie was saying.

"I was afraid that the tiny but indestructible part of me that has bowed down to white folks all of my life, the part that was born in the wombs of their slaves, the part that has seen my parents whipped by them and my children cower to them, I was afraid that tiny cell of bitterness, traced through the bloodline of my people, would divide and multiply inside me, and that nothing that I have with you, nothing that I share with you, not my feelings of love or loyalty or friendship or history, would be enough to keep it from clouding up my memories and filling up my heart."

She took a breath and went on.

"I was afraid that when I stepped off of the plane, the soles of my feet touching the soil of Africa, and landed on the place where we were born and knew as our home, the place we were stolen from, captured like animals and shipped here, I was afraid it would cause the feelings I had minimized and prayed over and held down for as long as I can remember to rise up, gather in my throat, and suffocate me."

There was a pause.

"That's why I was afraid."

The other women did not know how to respond. There was an uncomfortable silence as they struggled with an issue so strong and powerful that it threatened their friendship, an issue they could not dismantle, dissolve, or make disappear. They were suddenly painfully aware of the color of their skin, the thing that separated them.

Margaret turned the elephants around, all facing the front, a year unexpected. Beatrice gently put her cup and saucer back on the table, having kept it balanced on her knee for most of the conversation. Louise opened the top of the basket and found inside a pale pink stone resting on the bottom, rose quartz, she knew, the heart stone.

Charlotte put the stack of photographs on the floor beside her chair. She leaned toward Jessie, her white face drained and afraid. She asked, "And?" It was just that word, offered as a question, innocent but pleading.

"And, it didn't happen," she answered.

Charlotte sat back.

"I felt that the place had forgiven you." She continued. "I thought the ground would cry out like it did when Cain killed Abel, that it would demand your blood, your children's blood, my vow to despise you. But it didn't." She paused. "It sang."

Louise pulled out the small quartz stone and held it in the palm of her hand, noticing its lightness, its smooth pink shell. The other women watched as she rolled it between her fingers, thinking how it looked like the flat pads on the paws of a cat, the inside lip of a flower, the edge of the sky farthest from the setting sun, a blushing of clouds, surprised that a small thing could claim such color.

Louise passed the stone to Margaret, who held it closely to her eyes, noticing all its angles and textures. She then dropped it in Beatrice's hands, who rolled it across both sides of her face and gently touched it with the tip of her tongue, tasting the saltiness of sweat and the soil of Africa; then she passed it on to Charlotte.

The pastor held the rock in her hands, sliding it along the center of her palms, feeling its gloss and polish, and doubted that the earth was capable of such a difficult thing as forgiveness, an act that seemed to escape the hearts of most people.

She thought of the injustices people had done to the land, the mutilated rain forests and razed mountains, the torn ozone layer and the acid-lined clouds, the oil spills in the ocean and the shrinking deserts. She fingered the small stone and then gave it to Jessie.

"You really think it has the power to do that?" Charlotte asked. "That dust and springs of water and old trees can do such a thing?" She seemed unconvinced. "That the land can forgive savagery and the hands that chained and hanged and killed its children? Do you really think the earth has that much power or even the right to offer mercy to an enemy?"

Jessie took the stone and thought deeply before she answered. She considered what the young minister was asking, the depth of her question, the simplicity of what she had offered them. She too studied the small, pink stone, a rock mined from the quarries that were dug into the necks of brilliant hills, ravines cut into the valleys and severed from the forests.

She considered the hands of greedy engineers, the burdened backs of the workers, and the lined pockets of government officials, all collaborating to destroy the land and scar the earth just so one small pink rock might be uncovered and sold.

"I don't know if it has the right to give my mercy, my ancestors' forgiveness." She handed the quartz to Louise. "But it did it anyway."

She stood up to go into the kitchen and refill the teapot. The women waited.

"The grass and the shrub, the woodland and the savanna, the strands of wheat and the tender buds of cotton, the coffee beans and the desert scrub, they all had peace." She picked up the pot of tea and headed out of the room.

The four women slowly began flipping through the photographs and studying each other's gifts, contemplating the notion of forgiveness and whether their friend was as changed as she professed.

"And the land gave this peace to you?" Louise asked as Jessie returned to the room with a new pot of tea.

"Yes," Jessie replied. "The land, Africa, the ground of my people, the dirt that they brought buried beneath their fingernails and woven in their hair braids, the dirt they rubbed across their bodies as they were being roped and exiled, the dirt they had hidden in tiny leather bags that they wore around their necks along with the cold chains, this land, this earth, gave me peace."

She poured herself another cup of tea and held up the pot, an offer for anyone else who might want more.

Charlotte raised her cup and Jessie moved toward her.

"Well, I wish I had it," the preacher confessed as the older woman poured the tea in her cup. "I wish I could go somewhere and find that kind of peace. I wish my soul felt that unpolluted." She reached for the pitcher of milk.

Margaret handed it to her. "I don't know that you always have to travel to get it," she said to Charlotte. She thought of the recent peace she was only beginning to experience, the relief and the new ease with which she now faced life. "And it's not always about forgiveness," she added. "Sometimes it's about healing."

"Sometimes it comes," said Beatrice. "When you finally get the thing you never thought you'd get, when somebody trusts you." Beatrice turned toward Louise, who was facing her with a look of warmth and satisfaction.

"What do you think, Lou?" It was Jessie who asked.

"It came with acceptance for me, not from anybody else but from me, who I am, who I'll never be." Louise held out her cup to Jessie for more tea.

"I think peace comes when everything in a body and mind and soul is lined up, when the elements in a person's soul are sorted and undisputed," Beatrice added.

"And that takes what everybody's mentioned—trust, forgiveness, healing, acceptance." Margaret spoke to Charlotte. "And time."

"You're talking to a bunch of old women, Charlotte. It took us our whole lives to get where we are." Jessie poured the tea in Louise's cup and sat down next to her.

"You're young," Louise added. "A person doesn't find all her answers in the beginning." She thought of her own experiences, her own bereavement, her losses, her disappointments. "Sometimes it takes a while to figure out exactly what a heart needs to get uncluttered, and then it takes even longer to figure out how to make it happen."

"A lifetime," Beatrice said as she raised her cup.

Charlotte leaned against her seat and closed her eyes. She paid attention but was displeased with the suggestion. She wasn't interested in waiting thirty years to find peace.

Beatrice was sorting through the photographs, trying to figure out which stack of pictures went to Margaret and which stack went to the pastor, confused by the double direction of the photograph line, when the front door opened and Lana walked in. The women looked up.

"Oh, I'm sorry," she said as if she had broken up a meeting.

"It's all right, honey," Jessie replied. "We're just going through my pictures, hearing my stories." She did not speak of the suitcase her granddaughter-in-law tried to hide behind her legs.

The other women nodded their greetings.

"Here," Louise said to Beatrice as she leaned across the table and took the photographs from her friend, "give them to me." And Beatrice handed her both stacks.

"Would you like a cup of tea?" Jessie asked Lana.

"No, ma'am. Is Hope asleep?" She headed toward the bedroom.

"Yes. James put her down before he left for town." She studied the young woman, trying to understand if she was returning from somewhere she had been or if she was on her way to somewhere else.

"Did you have your exercise class?" she asked, remembering her weeknight schedule.

Lana nodded her head and walked out of the room. Margaret lifted her eyes up to Jessie. The two of them shared a look of concern, and Margaret got up from her seat and followed Lana to her bedroom. Louise continued flipping through the pictures.

"You okay?" Margaret asked the young woman as they stood in the hall.

Lana opened the door to the baby's room and peeked in. Hope was asleep. Her mother quietly closed the door. She faced Margaret and then walked to the rear of the house to the bedroom she and Wallace shared. The older woman followed.

"I wrote the letter almost two weeks ago," she said as she threw the suitcase on the bed and handed Margaret the unopened letter that was sitting on the dresser. "Got money out of the account, even bought an airline ticket."

Margaret shut the bedroom door.

"Tampa," she added. "I was going to Tampa."

Margaret leaned against the wall. She had no response.

"I picked today because Mr. and Mrs. Jenkins were home and I knew they would give Wallace a lot of support, help him with Hope and everything." She sat on the bed, knowing that the older woman was waiting for an explanation.

"I was standing at the boarding gate." She kicked off a shoe. "I was chosen to be screened by security." She paused, remembering how they asked her to step aside, how nervous she had been. "Of course they didn't find anything; and trust me, they looked." She said this with great animation.

Margaret smiled.

"But after they handed me back my suitcase, after I had

seen all my stuff taken out and handled by these strangers, after everything was replaced, I don't know." She pulled off her other shoe. "I started thinking about all the things I forgot to pack." She tugged at her socks.

"I didn't have sunscreen or tampons. I forgot my yellow sundress and that cute pair of sandals I bought at the end of summer last year." She pulled her long hair back and twisted it around her hand. "I just didn't have any of the right stuff," she concluded.

Then she looked down at her watch. "I'd be there now, had I gone. I drove around some before I came back."

There was a pause.

"Why did you come home?" the older woman asked. "You could have bought the things you needed when you got to Florida."

Lana turned around on the bed and examined her suitcase. "Tampa's already eighty degrees. I checked the weather before I left." She unzipped her bag and pulled out one of Hope's stuffed toys.

She twisted around to face Margaret. She thought before she spoke. "I don't know, Mrs. Peele. It just didn't seem like the right time to be gone, is all. I guess somehow thinking about flying into that heat made me long for a little more winter."

She got up from her bed, her daughter's toy in her hands. "It's her favorite; she probably missed it." She walked behind Margaret out of the room and down the hall.

Margaret stood at the door and watched as the young mother went into the room where her baby was sleeping. She heard the child being lifted from her crib, soft words quietly spoken, and then finally the sound of the creak and pull of a chair rocking back and forth.

The older woman left the bedroom, quietly passing the closed door, and returned to the den with her friends. She didn't ask for any more answers. Having left a marriage once herself, she understood that most of the time just the act of coming home is explanation enough.

She caught Jessie's eye as she sat down, her smile slight yet confident.

"Now, then," she asked, "what have I missed?"

"Just the pictures," Louise answered, handing her a pile.

"And the tea," Beatrice added as she took the teapot off the table and filled Margaret's cup.

"A few delicate moments of friendship," Jessie replied. "But we have plenty more of those." She took the pot of tea from Beatrice, placed it on the tray, and picked up another stack of photographs. "Yes," Margaret repeated, "plenty more of those."

Eleven

* A U N T * D O T ' S * H E L P F U L * H I N T S *

Dear Aunt Dot,
My car leaks oil. That's awful enough. The stain on my pants is worse. Help me save my favorite trousers!

Knee-Deep in Oil

Dear Knee-Deep,
Don't rub the stain. Blot and presoak the area with any spot cleaner and then wash the pants in hot water. Or you may want to try a professional for this one. Sometimes you just need to go outside your own cleaning solutions for help.

*A*re you sure it's full?" Charlotte stood behind the mechanic, leaning over him as he worked beneath the hood of her car.

"It's fine, see?" And he pulled out the dipstick and showed the minister the tip, which was black with oil completely up to the line that marked the tank as full.

She examined the stick as if she knew what it meant. "Well, okay, if you're sure." And she stepped away from him and walked around to examine her tires.

It was a cool autumn day, and the morning breeze stirred the dust at Charlotte's feet. "They got enough air, you think?"

The mechanic, a regular visitor at church, watched as the young woman moved around the car, scrutinizing the tires on her car. "Didn't you just get a new set?" he asked.

"A couple of months ago." She had circled to the front of the automobile. "So they should be all right?"

"Yes, ma'am, they should be fine." He used his handkerchief to shut the hood and then wiped his hands. His fingers were stained with grease.

He studied the minister.

"I never got to tell you, but that was a real nice service you had for Vastine last spring." Then he lifted his eyes and noticed all the cars and car owners waiting for his attention. "I hadn't ever been to one that was outside." He stuffed the handkerchief in his front pants pocket. "I think that's what I'd like to have too."

Charlotte nodded politely, opened the car door, and reached in for her purse. She handed the man her credit card to pay for the gas and the quart of oil and sat down in the driver's seat. As he left the car and walked inside the station, she closed her eyes and recalled the conversations she had had with Lamont and later Peggy when it was decided to have a graveside service for Vastine.

A warm day in spring, it had also been the day she had decided to resign.

After the anticipated death, arrangements were made. Even though Vastine's condition had been terminal for quite some time, there had never been any discussion about the funeral. So it wasn't until two days after the death that she met with the family to talk about what the service would entail.

When the pastor arrived at the house Lamont was by himself, the others having gone to the funeral home for a private viewing.

"Hey," Charlotte called out when she got out of the car and saw him sitting on the back steps. "How are you doing?"

"I could use a little something to deal with Mama." He was putting out a cigarette. "She is a pistol these days."

"You been to a meeting?"

"Last night," he answered. "I even told my story." He moved over so the young woman would have room to sit down. "Hey, I'm Lamont and I'm a junkie." He stuck out his hand for her to shake.

"Hey, Lamont." She smiled and sat down. She had been to AA meetings with her mother. "You staying clean?"

He faced her and shook his head at being asked again about his sobriety. "Clean and sober, three months, three weeks, and four days," he answered proudly.

Charlotte nodded in approval, but she knew that amount of time was no real record to rely upon. She knew that it took more than a couple of months to decide to stay on the wagon.

"Hey, you still taking sticks to the Cigarette Lady?" He glanced in the direction of her car.

"Why, you out?" She noticed the empty pack next to the door.

"Yeah. Grandma won't buy me cigarettes, and I ain't got paid this week."

Charlotte smiled and motioned toward her car. "It's unlocked."

Lamont walked to the car and found the cigarettes in the glove compartment. She noticed that he only took one, and she yelled at him, "Just take them all."

Lamont came back with the pack in his front shirt pocket. "You sure you don't want one?"

Charlotte laughed, shaking her head.

For a few minutes they sat on the steps without speaking. It was surprisingly warm, and she enjoyed the chance to be outside. Finally, she began the conversation.

"Where were you when he passed?" Charlotte had been there the entire day when Vastine died. Lamont's absence was clearly noticed.

"I had to work."

Charlotte knew that Lamont had been helping out a few days a week at the local car dealership washing cars and cleaning up the place. He and Peggy had decided that he needed to get out of the house once in a while. A friend had recommended him for the job.

"You didn't know he was dying?" Charlotte didn't mind asking the young man the hard questions. For some reason, she was comfortable with him in a way she wasn't with the other church members.

He shifted uncomfortably. "Yeah, I knew he was dying."

Charlotte waited for more.

He lit a cigarette and flipped the used match in the old cup he had beside him.

"I made my peace with Granddaddy a week ago." He did not hesitate to answer. "We said our good-byes."

Charlotte slid her hands up and down the sides of her arms. "You want to talk about it?"

He blew out the smoke. "Not really," he answered. "Why, you wanting to be all preacherlike and help me with my grief?"

She laughed at that. "I'm just saying you can talk about it if you want to."

He shook his head. "I've done a lot of stuff wrong," he replied. "I'm working on all that, trying to get right." He took a long hard draw. "But I don't feel bad about things here."

He balanced the cigarette between his fingers. "Me and Pop, we were cool." He looked away from the minister, stretching his long legs out in front of him.

Charlotte watched Lamont as he spoke.

"I sat up with him every night the week before he died. He was a little scared of the dark." Lamont turned to face the pastor. "We talked about a lot of things." He tapped his cigarette beside the steps where they were sitting. "His mind was sharp all the way up until a couple of days before he died. He told me a lot of stories about when he was young, how he lost his business one time and went bankrupt."

Charlotte realized she had never heard this story about her parishioner, and she became interested.

"He said a man gets a lot of chances to mess up his life, and he gets just as many to make things right." Lamont took another draw off the cigarette and waited before blowing out the smoke.

"I don't know if that's true or not." He studied Charlotte to see if she would answer. When she didn't, he continued. "I do know that if I do anything right it's because of them." He motioned with his chin toward the house. Charlotte understood he meant his grandparents. "They make me think I can do better."

Charlotte watched a flock of swallows as they flew high above their heads. A black cloud dancing, they moved steadily across the sky. There was a pause in the conversation and she considered the power of love.

"So how is your mom doing, really?" she asked.

"She's cried and made a lot of noise, but I guess she knew he was going to die."

Charlotte nodded.

"I worry about Granny, though, her being here all by herself."

"You're here, aren't you?"

The young man faced the minister. "My trial's in less than a month," he answered. "The lawyer asked for extra time because of everything, but all that hasn't gone away just because I'm trying to do better." He finished the cigarette and put it out in his makeshift ashtray.

"No, I guess not," she said. She thought she heard a car in the driveway. "Well, why don't you wait to cross that bridge when you come to it?" she added.

"Wait to cross that bridge?" he asked grinning. "You can't come up with anything better than, 'wait to cross that bridge'? That's the best you got? What kind of sorry preacher are you?"

Charlotte elbowed the young man and they laughed together. And when Peggy and the others drove up, the young pastor was feeling good about things in the DuVaughn household, pleased that Lamont had found peace at the home of his grandparents and that he was straightening himself out. She was even angry at herself that she had considered asking him about the missing CD player.

After everyone got out of the car, Peggy invited the pastor inside. The others stayed on the porch with Lamont while Peggy and Charlotte went into the kitchen and began discussing the funeral. The young minister pulled out her pad of paper to write things down that Peggy wanted to have in the funeral service. Charlotte had merely assumed that since the DuVaughns had been active church members most of their lives it would be a typical church funeral service. She had already notified the musician and the choir, asking for volunteers to sing. She had already designed the bulletin and had contacted the janitor to make sure the sanctuary was clean and in good order.

Because of Peggy's age and her more conservative leanings and since it was only early spring and the weather was so unpredictable, Charlotte had never imagined that her parishioner would want a nontraditional service, held completely outside at the graveside. She had never considered that Peggy had already made such a definite decision.

"Did Vastine ask for a short service?" Charlotte, still unsuspecting, asked the widow as they watched Lamont talking to his mother and aunts outside the window.

Peggy nodded her head, but it was obvious to the minister that there was more to the story than just a dead man's request. She also found it odd that the dying man had never mentioned it to her since they had often talked about matters of importance to him.

"Is this what the family wants?" She knew something wasn't right, and she kept pushing for the real answer.

Peggy slowly nodded her head again, still watching her family on the steps outside and still unwilling to explain.

It wasn't that Charlotte had been against the outside service. She actually preferred the more intimate funerals, the ones without all the pomp and circumstance. But the nontraditional idea seemed artificial somehow, as if it was forced upon Peggy, unchosen by the family, placed upon them by somebody else.

"Has anybody said anything to you?" she finally asked the

older woman. "Did somebody say something about Lamont?"

"His trial's in a couple of weeks," Peggy responded, her
face expressionless. "I'm so glad they were able to postpone
it, with the funeral and everything."

Charlotte sat in silence, waiting to hear more. The parishioner answered phone calls and kept going outside to speak
to her daughters. The pastor waited through lunch and visi-
tors, a conversation with the funeral home personnel and the
departure of the grandson. She was determined to hear more
from Peggy about the reason for her decision.

Finally, when the children went out to buy their father a
shirt and tie and the house grew uncomfortably quiet, Peggy
sat down at the kitchen table next to her pastor and confessed.

"Grady and Bill Stevens came over a couple of months ago."
She kept her eyes lowered while she explained. "Not long
after Lamont came home," she said. "They said they had talked
to the hospice nurse." She shook her head as if she still had
trouble accepting what had happened. "They called the main
office and told the head nurse that Lamont had a drug problem and that they should make sure they kept an eye on him."

The older woman was tired. "Everybody acted so different after that." She pulled apart the tissue she had in her
hands. "They started counting the pills, asking me all these
questions about Lamont being alone with Vastine, about
whether I had noticed changes in my grandson's behavior,
when he was going back to jail."

The tears filled her eyes. "I felt like a criminal." She reached to her face with part of the tissue and wiped her eyes. "No, worse, I felt like an imbecile. The nurses and Grady, the women from the church who visited, the social worker, they all treated me like I couldn't take care of myself or Vastine and like Lamont was going to rob us blind or take all of Vastine's drugs."

Charlotte did not know what to say. The words felt like hail stinging her skin, her eyes. She wanted to run for cover. She was angry at the church members and angry that Peggy had not told her before now.

"He's a good boy," the older woman added, trying not to cry. "He's been working so hard since he got home." And then without another word she took on an air of resolution, walked out of the room, and returned with a list of her chosen pallbearers and a couple of songs she wanted to have sung at her husband's grave.

"I just would rather not go inside," she said as she handed her pastor the paper.

And Charlotte took the list of requests without having anything more to add.

After spending most of the day with the DuVaughn family, Charlotte went home and in anger wrote a letter of resignation, announcing her disapproval of the church members' behavior, her shame at being their pastor, and her relief at the thought of no longer having to serve them. She wrote it and almost delivered it but waited, deciding instead to talk to her counselor about it before she went through with her plans.

Charlotte sat in her car, waiting for the mechanic to return. She checked her watch and wondered if something was wrong with her credit card. She looked around the station but didn't see the man. She leaned back and remembered the session she'd had with Marion. It was a clear memory since she had never seen her counselor appear so provoked.

To her surprise, Marion had not supported her decision but rather had informed her that such an act was unprofessional, knee-jerk, and beneath the young woman's character. "This can't be the reason you leave," the therapist had said, her criticism sharp and unswerving. "You've got some very important people in that congregation, people who have nurtured you and loved you, people you have loved."

With that, Charlotte thought of the cookbook committee, Nadine, a few others.

"You owe them more than just this angry letter. You owe them an explanation, and I'm not sure you have a clear one, even for yourself."

Marion was very directed, very focused.

"Why are you leaving the ministry?" she asked pointedly.

Charlotte felt the tears gather and fall.

"Because I can't believe they treated Lamont this way. I can't believe that they would make a woman memorialize her husband outside because she didn't feel welcome in her church anymore." The words choked in her throat.

"You never took away her welcome. That group of women you socialize with never took away her welcome.

Nobody made your parishioner feel that way." She stopped and started again.

"Granted, those men had no right to do what they did, but they did not represent the entire church. You've said yourself that the others in the congregation rallied around this family, especially in the end."

Then the counselor sat up in her chair and leaned into her client. "And really, Charlotte, you were actually shocked by how they responded to this young man? Come on," she said, resting her chin in her hands, "you're not that naive about church folks, are you?"

Charlotte turned away. "No," she whispered. "I know; I've known." She hesitated, examining herself for answers. Then she glanced up and noticed the picture of the gardener, the one her therapist had kept on her wall for years.

She looked over the painting, recalling how much purpose and direction it had brought her through the past couple of years. Then she spoke of her pain again.

"I'm just tired of everything feeling so barren all the time. I'm tired of planting seeds and watching the ground, and adding a little water and watching the ground, and putting on some fertilizer and watching the ground, and never seeing anything. I'm tired of chopping the weeds and dancing around flat dirt and tending and never seeing anything. I just need more."

There was a pause between the two women.

"What about your father?" Marion asked at that point.

Charlotte was taken aback by an attempt to connect the two situations.

"What do you mean?" she asked.

"Have you had any more dreams?" Marion responded.

Charlotte considered her recent nightly rest, the pictures in her mind, the journaling, but she remembered nothing new. She couldn't think of a new stage in her dream analysis. She shook her head.

"So, according to your dreams, you still have not reunited with your father, you've still not gotten together? You always manage to get sidetracked, and he's still an enormous, looming figure in the scenes?"

Charlotte thought about the question, having had no recent dream to consider. The previous ones had all been similar—her father, a larger-than-life presence, unapproachable, unavailable, somewhere in the scene, while Charlotte was always involved in some sort of decision-making process, some distraction, something that kept her from going to her dad.

"Why do you think you can never get to your father?" Marion asked.

"I don't know," the pastor answered.

Marion waited, but there was no other response.

She answered her own question. "Is it possible that you're afraid that if you do finally get to him, finally find your way to him, that you'll discover that he really isn't the man you think he is? That he didn't just turn you and your sister down when you needed him because he was busy or uncaring but rather because he really wouldn't have been able to change the way things went anyway?" She seemed reluctant but determined to analyze her client's dreams. "Is it possible that just as you have been gravely disappointed in the men in your church, in the institution itself, that you've stayed away from your father all these years because you've worried that you'll be gravely disappointed in him?"

Charlotte was confused. "But I've already been disappointed in him. When I needed him, he turned me down. How could I be more disappointed than that?" She sincerely wanted answers.

"Yes," Marion replied, "you were disappointed then." She did not even notice that their designated time together had passed. "But I think there may still be a part of you that believes that if he had taken the two of you, if he had been in the home, if he had done anything, life would have been different." She spoke delicately, gently, the words a quiet possibility.

"I wonder if you haven't given your father magical properties, made him bigger than he really is." She took a breath. "And the truth is, maybe life would have been different. Maybe Serena wouldn't have died, maybe your mother would have gotten sober a lot earlier."

She stopped briefly and then continued. "But maybe nothing would have been different. Maybe there still would have been heartbreak and sorrow and death. Maybe your father is no more than just a man and would have been unable to change the course of events in your family's life, even if he'd had wanted to, even if he'd tried."

Charlotte's mind was reeling. Images from her dreams flashed, pictures of her father, and she suddenly recalled snippets of a recent conversation she'd had with Bea. The older woman had come to see her to talk about her husband's struggle after having learned something about his brother's past. "He was so let down," she had said. "So disappointed in him."

"But what does that have to do with the church?" Charlotte asked, trying to shake off the muddled memories.

Marion waited to explain, letting her client catch up to what had been shared.

"Maybe your expectations of church folks, your hopes and desires, as genuine and admirable as they are, maybe they're just a little higher than can be realized." She studied her client.

"People are people, in church or out of church. We go forward one step and back three. Your father, the deacon, the teenager in trouble, your women friends, everybody deserves grace."

Marion was silent for a while, collecting her thoughts, appearing as if she wanted to finish with just the right thing.

"Write your letter if you feel it is time to leave, but make sure you are clear that this is not a reactionary decision, that this is not a choice based upon the behavior of a couple of men, that this is a decision about *your* heart, *your* desires, *your* needs."

And this part she said with a lot of strength: "Don't kill what may be happening underground, growth that may be occurring where you can't see it; don't destroy that with your bitterness. You owe them that. Make it plain," she said, remembering the phrase often used by preachers. "Keep it clean." And then time was called. Charlotte's session was over.

So Charlotte had waited. She had waited for more than six months. She had talked to Jessie and Margaret and Louise and Beatrice, separately and together. She had gone to Grady and to the deacon board to express her disappointment and to Peggy to express her apologies for how members of the church had behaved.

She had spoken of her anger and dealt with it. There were even a few of the deacons who said that they were sorry, several who surprised her with their remorse. Peggy, the most astonishing one of all, made amends with those from whom she felt estranged.

The pastor had tied up loose ends. She had gone with Lamont to his trial and spoken in court as a character witness. The missing CD player had strangely reappeared in her office; she still didn't know where it had been or who had taken it. She had visited the young man in prison, sharing in the disappointment of his long sentence but promising to visit again.

She had encouraged Lana and Wallace to get into counseling, helping them find a suitable therapist. She had been with Dick when his brother died. She continued to work on her issues with Marion, and finally, when spring and summer had passed and autumn was fast approaching, she felt it was time to go: Charlotte sat in her car and remembered leaving.

On her last Sunday there was a potluck dinner in the church fellowship hall after the service. The tables were filled with all the foods the Hope Springs church was known for. Chicken pie, barbecue, pinto beans, turnip greens, sweet potato casserole. Charlotte stood at the door and watched as the women hurried in and out of the kitchen, removing the lids of pots and dishes and placing serving spoons beside them.

She thought of the cookbook the church women had put together, the pride and family histories measured and offered in the recipes they submitted. She recounted the first meeting about the book, the excitement of some and the indifference of others, the give-and-take process always a part of community projects. She studied the women as they moved about the fellowship hall, their confidence in their ability to cook and serve, the secure sense of themselves that always emerged when food was involved. She thought of their lives of service and nurture, their quiet ways of affection, and appreciated how far they all had come in the past three years, the friendships, the trust, the surprise of intimacy.

She watched as some of the men filled cups with ice while others searched for chairs and pushed them beneath the tables, the banter that played between them, the teamwork, the camaraderie, the unified effort to prepare a place to eat.

She watched the children sneak past mothers and grandmothers, snatching up samples, and she remembered why she loved this place, remembered why she had come and stayed. Even if church folks mess up everything else, she thought, they always know how to feed one another.

"Sure hope you're hungry," Beatrice said as she sped past Charlotte to place her prune cake next to the pies and cookies.

"She still thinks you might have a kink or two in need of loosening," Louise said as she came up behind the pastor.

"Does anybody ever eat that cake?" Charlotte asked.

"Actually," Louise replied as she walked over to the table with her bowl of green beans and then returned to stand next to Charlotte, "it really isn't awful." Then she smiled as she watched her friend bark orders to the other women in the kitchen. "And it does have a way of working things out." She put her arm around the young woman.

Peggy DuVaughn came in the side door, and Charlotte noticed that it was Grady who stopped pouring the iced tea and walked over to hold open the door for the widow as she moved inside. The pastor could not hear the conversation, but she saw the deacon speak a few words and reach up to take her dish. Peggy held it out to him, and just as he took it Charlotte noticed that he squeezed the back of her hand. And they stood that way, a brief and tenuous moment of reconciliation, until Hope crawled past Lana and Wallace and bumped into the back of Grady's legs. They both looked down at the little girl and laughed, the moment past but not forgotten.

It was all just as it should have been, laughter, stories, too much to eat, and the lingering notion that sitting together around the table and enjoying food and fellowship make the best memories of church. The young pastor recognized in her farewell dinner, in her reception of the gift of being fed by those she had served, that even though their journey together had felt like they had merely stumbled forward at times, gone backward at others, still somehow they had managed a little progress. There had been a bit of knowledge gained, a little hope stored. And Charlotte was at peace that pastor and church had walked together. They had cried and wearied and prayed and laughed and eaten and been filled and walked together.

They wished her well as she traveled to visit her father and then to the Southwest where she had taken a job as director of a women's shelter. It had all seemed quite appropriate to everyone. And even though it was lovely and pleasant and meaningful, an event of self-understanding and acceptance, it was not, however, the real celebration of good-bye. It was not the one she would hold in her heart. Her friends had planned that one.

On the first weekend of autumn, a cool September day, the cookbook committee took their pastor to a labyrinth garden somewhere south of Atlanta, Georgia. Louise and Beatrice had suggested it, deciding that this would be the best place for them to say good-bye.

And so it was that late that evening, under a night sky filled with stars and a round white moon, the women walked the garden path, hands held and silent. The older women had written prayers for their young friend, and when they quietly approached the end of the labyrinth, standing in the center, surrounded by large decorative pots filled with rose glow and purple sage and gathered around a mosaic of colored stones pressed into the earth, the face of a woman, each of them read her petition.

"Health and wholeness," Margaret said as she placed a small strand of purple beads around Charlotte's left wrist.

"Acceptance," added Louise as she handed the young woman a scarred but still beautiful conch shell she had found at the beach many years earlier.

"Home," Jessie had prayed. "Give this child a home." And she placed at her feet a small glass bottle filled with dirt collected from two continents.

"And peace," Beatrice had prayed the final prayer. "A clean heart."

She stepped forward with a small pink rose quartz like the one Jessie had brought back from Africa for Louise. It was shaped like a heart with a hole in the top. A string of brown leather was pulled through, long enough to fit over the young woman's head. And as she draped the necklace around Charlotte's neck, the women had all gathered closer.

A fountain flowed nearby, the sound of running water a cleansing reminder to Charlotte of her childhood baptism.

"We are forever friends," Jessie said, the words like fingers dipped in cool water, wet upon her brow.

"That means we will always care for you, always be there for you," Margaret added, remembering the significance of her friendship.

"We will always wish the best for you, always want only good things for you." Louise reached up and wiped a tear from Charlotte's eye.

"What we have we share with you and you will always remain in our hearts." Beatrice cupped the pastor's face in her hands.

"Forever friends," Charlotte repeated. And the words had been a benediction.

And there in the garden, surrounded by the women who had birthed her in faith, raised her to her womanness, and helped untangle her from sadness, she found a way to depart, her soul with wings, wide and strong and opening into a string of long, clean days.

"Sorry it took me so long. Our machine broke." The mechanic reached into the car and handed Charlotte the credit card form to sign.

"So, you're leaving Hope Springs," he said, noticing all the boxes in the backseat and remembering the news of her resignation.

She wrote her signature without response. Then she tore off her copy and handed the form back to the mechanic. "A person never really leaves Hope Springs, does she?" She reached for her sunglasses and strapped on her seat belt.

He stepped away from the car, smiled, and shook his head. "Nah, I guess not," he said.

And the young pastor checked her mirrors to see behind her, turned her head left and right, then faced straight ahead.

She dropped down her visor, touched the pink stone she wore around her neck, pulled away from the service station, and headed west.